THE
OF FORGOTTEN MEMORIES

"The key to the present lays hidden in the past."

by

FEDERICO CHINI

All characters appearing in this work are fictitious. Any resemblance to real persons, living or dead, is purely coincidental.

Cover design by Federico Chini

First Printing: May 2011

Il-baħar żaqqu ratba u rasu iebsa.
The sea has a soft belly and a hard head.
(Maltese proverb)

Maltese Islands
Zebbug
Marsalforn
Xaghra
Ta Pinu
Nadur
Victoria (Rabat)
G O Z O
Dwejra
Qala Point
Mgarr Harbour
Ta' Cenc
Xlendi
COMINO
MALTA
ITALY
Sicily
Mediterranean Sea
Maltese Islands

FOREWORD

When I returned to the island of Gozo, the house where my family and I had once lived was gone, transformed into an apartment block with little character and lots of cement.

Determined to live by the coast in a place that could bring memories of my childhood, I asked around for an old house for sale at a good price.

It took a few months for the right house to come on the market. A cousin of mine informed me of a house for sale just next to the port, in the little alley that led to the church.
"It's one of the oldest houses in the bay," he said "the old fisherman who used to live in it died less than a year ago. He left no heirs but the church."
"It will need some refurbishing" he warned me "but once finished, it will be just what you are dreaming of."

He was right. It was exactly the kind of house I had been dreaming of; it had high ceilings, thick walls, arched doorways and a small, stone staircase that spiraled all the way to the roof.

I bought it.

A few weeks later, as I was scraping off the paint in one of the smaller rooms on the first floor, to my surprise, jammed between two limestone bricks, I found a tiny little treasure.

It was a small, white piece of paper that the years had turned yellow and the air had faded out. It had been lying in that crack in the wall for many years, stuck in the fissure between two bricks, folded in four and hidden by a layer of white paint that had stiffened its edges.
Inside the paper, written in elegant handwriting that curled around like waves on the shoreline, were a few sentences. The words seemed part of a poem, which talked of whispering people and spying eyes.

Those words became my little gateway to the life of the Muscat family.

PART I - Fire

CHAPTER 01

THE MISSING BOATS.

The most tragic memory in the recent history of the island of Gozo was without any doubt the tragedy of the 30th of October 1948.
That day, the southwesterly wind, that the Maltese people call *Lbiċ*, had been blowing with all its strength for most of the day. The sea was rough and by the early afternoon, the ferry that linked the island of Malta to neighbouring Gozo had suspended its operations, leaving many Gozitans stranded on the main island.
It was the eve of a long weekend and the desire to return home kept many waiting at the port. Eventually, despite the weather, the owner of a large *luzzu* decided to attempt the crossing. The news spread fast and in no time, twenty-five people crammed aboard the vessel.

It was evening when the boat finally put out to sea.

The first part of the journey went smoothly. Sheltered by the coastline of the islands, the vessel sailed towards its destination without any problems, but as it passed the small island of Comino the waves began crashing onto the boat with violence.
Seeing the danger, the captain suggested changing course to head towards a more sheltered bay but many argued that they'd rather keep sailing to the main port were they could find means of transport to get to their homes. And so it was.
Needless to say, it was the wrong decision.

A few minutes later, as the over-crammed *luzzu* sailed along the narrow channel between the islands of Gozo and Comino, tragedy struck. Hit by a bigger wave, the boat reared up, then capsized.
With the coast lying just a hundred yards away, men and women tried to swim towards it, but the currents were so strong and the sea so rough that reaching the shore was almost impossible.
Only three men eventually managed to reach the island. A fourth one made it to a small rock where he remained perched for many hours waiting for rescue. The other twenty-one all perished.

11th October 1980

Fanal was the first one to notice the missing boats.

To everyone in the little port of Marsalforn, Saviour Bonnici was better known as *Tal-Fanal*, a nickname he had earned after the war, when night fishing using a huge lamp which some said was as visible as the beam of the *Fanal Ta' Ġordan*, the local lighthouse.
An old man, *Fanal* lived in a small house by the church and passed his days sitting by the port watching the boats go out to sea.
In summer, if the sun was not too hot, he sat on one of the port's benches, beneath the shadow of a tamarisk tree. In winter, he observed the port through the glass door of his son's restaurant, just across the street from the port.
Not many knew that he had fought in both world wars. At the age of twenty-four he had fought the Germans for the control of the Jutland peninsula in Denmark and

twenty-five years later, he had helped smuggles Maltese refugees from Sicily back to the Maltese Islands.
In the port, everyone had heard about the time *Fanal*'s boat had hit a floating mine, killing a refugee who had just regained his freedom. That night, they had sailed with no moon and all lights turned off for fear of being spotted by a German *Messerschmitt.* They had sailed quietly, following the stars and praying to be invisible, but as the first light brightened the horizon, a mine had shattered the silence. The boat had sunk at once, taking down with her one of the two rescued men. *Fanal* and two other men had swum for hours. When they eventually reached the coast they were so exhausted that they collapsed on the beach.

Nowadays there was little left of the man who had fought against the Germans and crossed the Mediterranean on a little boat guided only by the stars. The man who sat day after day on the same restaurant chair, observing the fishermen going out to sea with his tired eyes, was a curved man, thin and bony, with missing teeth and shaking hands.
His voice was like a croaking hiss, which often exploded in a violent laugh and mostly ended in a harsh coughing fit.

That morning, looking out of his kitchen window, he had seen the storm heading towards the islands, had felt the moist air brought by the *grigal* wind and had observed the dark clouds mounting over the horizon.

When the rain started, *Fanal* was sitting in his son's restaurant.
The fishermen were returning to port and one by one boats were pulled safely ashore, leaving the little harbour empty like a bowl of water. It was just before the storm

reached the bay that *Fanal* realised that two boats had not yet returned.

"They're not back yet!" he shouted to his son who stood behind the counter.
"Who's not back?" replied his son.
"The Muscats."
Fanal then stood up from his chair, removed the woollen rug from his legs and walked to the glass door. Outside the rain poured down, washing the port's grey tarmac and tinting the sea surface with mud.
Opening the door, a cold gust of wind crept past him. Ignoring it, *Fanal* squinted and searched the horizon for the two missing boats. All he saw was a dark mass of clouds that the wind kept pushing towards the islands.

CHAPTER 02

THE STORM.

It takes just one wave to capsize a boat, and one more to take it down.

11th October 1980

The very first lightning seemed to strike as far away as Italy; its gleam lit up a small slice of horizon brightening enough of the grey sky to reveal the familiar shape of the *Anna Marija.* Then the clouds coughed a distant thunder and the fishing boat blended back into the pouring rain.

Karmenu Muscat smiled with renewed hope. He muttered something to the wind then keeping his one good eye to the sea, he corrected the boat's course to follow his brother's.

The Muscat's fleet was made up of just three men on two small boats, Karmenu, aboard the *Ħamra,* and Ġorġ and his son Dwardu aboard the *Anna Marija.* Like most Maltese boats, both vessels were *luzzus*, almond shaped boats build in solid wood and painted in bright colours.

The Muscats had been roughly ten miles from the islands when the storm had reached them.

According to the weather forecast, the storm was due to have swept past Sicily and continued westwards towards the northern coast of Tunisia but at some point during the early morning the winds had shifted and the storm had changed its course, heading directly towards the little Maltese archipelago.

The first drops of rain had arrived without any warning when the darker clouds were still far away and the island of Gozo was still in full sight. Then the wind had grown to a gale, the gloomiest part of the horizon had swooped fast over the water and the storm had then closed in fast. Vertical, black clouds had towered over over the little Muscat's fleet surrounding them. The island had disappeared and the sea started mounting.

Pushed by the power of their inboard engines, the two *luzzus* had traveled side by side heading towards land, then, forced apart by the swelling sea, they had taken different courses.
For a while, they had sailed blindly, looking for each other like sightless people lost in a desert, then they had given up.

Peering through the pouring rain, Karmenu waited for lightning to strike and once again reveal the position of his brother's boat. It arrived a little later, crossing the sky like a spider-web and lashing into the sea.
The *Anna Marija* emerged from the greyness but it was further away than he had expected. Too far.
He was losing them.

At the age of forty-six, Karmenu Muscat was an experienced seaman. In his life he had twice experienced the full power of a storm at sea and both times had survived unscathed. But the island where he lived was full of stories of fishermen who had not been as lucky. The most recent of them was about a man called Xerri, who five years earlier had gone out at sea never to return.

October was the month of sudden thunderstorms that lashed the sea and battered the countryside, and this year was proving to be no exception.

Karmenu frowned at the greyness that surrounded him. The waves were mounting, the lightning was getting closer and the rain was pouring with so much intensity that the bottom of the boat was slowly filling up.
He could no longer search for his brother's boat. It was time to head back to the port.

CHAPTER 03

DWARDU MUSCAT.

Aboard the *Anna Marija*, Dwardu checked the level of diesel left in the tank. There was enough fuel to reach the port without any problem, he thought.
"Still half a tank" he shouted to his father at the front of the boat. His father nodded in return.
They both knew they could also rely on an extra gallon of diesel stored in the front compartment.

The rain was pouring over them and waves were mounting.

Half an hour had passed since the last time they'd seen the *Ħamra*. All around was one big, grey shadow.

Twenty-two year old Dwardu Muscat had been at sea for most of his life. He had started fishing at the age of ten, had dropped out of school four years later and that same year he had started his life as a full time fisherman with his father and his uncle.

The storm was still hovering over their heads and the sea was boiling beneath them.

Peering through the oilskin's hood, Dwardu tried to see some sign of land. He reckoned they were less than a few miles from the western tip of the Gozo, but the rain was so thick that he could barely see the end of the boat.

Then he saw something.

"*Madunna*!" he swore. It was no land, but a wave bigger than any he had seen in a long time.

He stood up to size the danger.

"*Ar'hemm! Ġejja wahda kbira!* There is a big one coming!" he warned his father at the front of the boat, but his voice died away in the wind. His legs buckled.

The wave before him was already mounting, it was a wall of water, mighty and fearsome, higher than the boat's hull, steep and menacing. But what shook him was not only that wave but the following ones which were even bigger and fiercer.

Following what he had learned during his years at sea, Dwardu approached the swell at a forty-five degree angle, veering the boat to climb the wave's side.

Once the vessel reached the top of the wave, Dwardu pushed the keel to cut the frothing crest. Unexpectedly, the small *luzzu*, glided over the swell and with the grace of a dancer then started its descent.

Breathing a sigh of relief, Dwardu repeated the same manoeuvre a second time. The boat climbed the second wave with ease and slid past it.

Then the third wave arrived.

If the first wave had been a wall, this one looked like a mountain. Its razor edge crest and powerful flanks were like whale slamming its tail.

With his eyes to its crest, Dwardu thrust the boat over the wave's flank once again. The boat reached the top of the wave then lost its speed.

Dwardu shot a quick glance in the direction of his father and saw him reaching for the mooring rope. As the boat reared up, it hung in the air for a moment then plummeted with violence onto the surface of the sea.

The impact was so hard that the boat creaked as if it was about to shatter in pieces.
The right sideboard, which had always fitted loosely was hurled into the sea. Along with it went one of the twined fishing lines that rested on the right groove, an empty tank and few floats.
The rest of the objects aboard the boat clattered in fear, then remained silent.

Regaining control of the vessel, Dwardu felt lucky to be still in one piece and a quick glance at the front of the boat assured him that his father was fine too.
It was then that the *Anna Marija* quivered for a second time. A strange noise exhaled from its engine, then, as the noise blended back into the grumbling sound of the waves, the engine rattled and suddenly died.

CHAPTER 04

ĠORĠ MUSCAT

As the engine stopped and the "*Anna Marija*" started fluttering over the waves in an awkward silence, Ġorġ and Dwardu held each other's eyes for a moment then they both moved towards the engine.

One of the large stones that they used as anchor had rolled onto the side of the motor.

Dwardu's father, Ġorġ Muscat was a thin man, with wiry hands and bony shoulders. His balding head was hidden beneath a blue woollen hat, his eyes were dark and patient, and his face was covered by a thick black beard that spread evenly from his cheeks to his chin, full and round like a terrier's muzzle.

Of the two, Ġorġ seemed the calmest, confident that if something was wrong with the boat he would be able to fix it.

Ġorġ had built the *Anna Marija* with his own hands over thirty years earlier, and it had taken him the best part of five years.
The war had just finished and the Maltese economy was at its lowest point in years. Children went hunting for sparrows to eat and able workers emigrated to Australia to work on new railway tracks.
Ġorġ too had considered moving abroad but when his father had died his plans had changed.

With no pension for widows or orphans, his mother had found it hard to make ends meet. For a few months, they survived thanks to the help of better-off relatives, then the church had taken them under their wing helping them with clothes and food in return for small chores. That summer, Ġorġ worked at the port, helping fishermen mend their nets, sell fish and repair boats but the money was scarce and irregular.
Just as he had set his mind to emigrate to Australia, Ġorġ had found his first real job, working full time in one of the island's boatyards, building and repairing traditional boats for the local fishermen's fleet. It was a hard job, but Ġorġ liked it. Hours were long, but the work varied and the money was good.

Three summers later, he was a skilled carpenter, able to understand and adapt the plans of a *luzzu*, to saw and plane a keel, to scarf the bottom ribs and fit the crankshaft of an inboard engine.

One evening, coming back from the boatyard, Ġorġ sat by the port and watched the fishermen return from the sea with boxes full of fish. What a display! He had forgotten his father's sense of pride as he returned from a day out at sea and displayed his catch to the people swarming the port.
"It's like a game", he used to say, "you first show the small fish, then the catch of the day, then all the rest".

It was then that Ġorġ decided that he was going to build his own boat and continue his family trade. After all, his father had been a fisherman and his grandfather before him.

Without leaving his carpentry job, he began equipping the family shed with a few simple tools which he bought second hand from the market. Then came the sketch; he

modeled it on one of the local *luzzu*, the boat he considered the best on the island.
With a piece of string first and a folding ruler later, he measured each part of the boat, writing down every proportion first on paper, then on the walls of the family shed.
He worked alone, patiently, evening after evening. Sometimes his brother Karmenu helped him but he wasn't cut out for it. With his one good eye he found it hard to keep the right measure. So it was only Ġorġ who stayed late at night, often sleeping in the shed so he could resume working in the early morning before going to the boatyard.

It took him almost four years to put together the boat's hull, two more months to fit the engine, the shaft and the propeller and three more weeks to paint the boat with two coats of red, blue and white paint on the outside and two coats of green on the inside.

Once finished the boat he quit his job at the shipyard and became a fisherman.

Ġorġ crawled towards the engine, praying for the damage to be repairable.

With the left side of his back throbbing with pain, he started dragging the stone away from the engine. He rolled it over the bottom boards then secured it with a rope at the front of the boat.
Dwardu drew closer to the engine to inspect the damage.
Both fishermen knew that without the thrust of the engine they were as powerless as a seagull without wings.

At first glance they saw no meaningful damage. The wooden box that protected the most delicate parts of the engine seemed to have absorbed most of the impact, leaving just a dust mark as evidence of the contact.

Without giving it more thought, Dwardu clutched the starting-handle with both hands, he looked at his father and started coiling the rope around the pan.
"I'll try to restart it!" he said.
Rivulets of rain and sweat kept running down his face.
His father nodded.
Closing his eyes, Dwardu spun the metal bar with all his strength and yowled. He then waited for the familiar rumbling sound to start but the engine just coughed a deep metallic noise and died again.

Again Dwardu whirled the starting handle. The engine wheezed, but nothing more.

"We should have bought a second engine!" said Dwardu, his voice betraying a trace of rancour.
The two of them had discussed the possibility of adding a second engine to the *'Anna Marija'* many times before. Dwardu insisted that newer boats were equipped with two engines, a main engine, with the propeller in the centre of the stern and an emergency one with a smaller screw on the side of the hull.
But fitting a second engine to the *'Anna Marija'* would have meant changing much more than the boat could bear.

They tried to start the engine one more time, but again, with no success.

"It's the transmission," said Ġorġ, "no," he corrected himself, "it's the screw."

It was the worst nightmare of any fisherman: debris getting stuck in the propeller, blocking the screw.

The rain kept pouring onto them and the waves shook them like leaves in the wind.

Moving to the stern of the boat, Dwardu removed the rudder and looked down at the screw.
White dashes of water bubbled at each swell.
Holding tight to the boat's edge, he leaned further and peeked below the surface of the water.
He saw his father was right, a wooden was board sticking out of the propeller, its yellow surface glaring through the water like a *lampuka* hiding beneath the boat.
"The sideboard," he shouted, "it got stuck in the screw!"

For a few minutes, Dwardu tried to reach the sideboard with his hands, leaning over the boat's stern and battling the waves, but it was well beyond his reach.

"Try this." Said his father handing over the boathook.
The boat hook was as old as the boat, its wooden shaft smoothed by the years and its hook rusted to a sombre brown colour. Dwardu plunged it beneath the boat and directed it onto the wooden plank. He pushed hard against the sideboard, stretching himself as far as he could, trying to disentangle the wooden board from the engine's screw. But their attempt to revive the engine had pushed the wooden board even further onto the propeller.

As the boat rocked with each wave, Dwardu felt the boat's frame press deeper into his ribcage. He tried a while longer then gave up.

Heaving himself back into the boat he found his father looking into the storm, his yellow hood deep over his forehead so that his black beard was split by the hood's fastening-lace.

The centre of the storm was getting closer.
Then a bolt of lightning cut the air close to the boat and a loud thunderclap pealed through the air.

CHAPTER 05

SARAH.

Marsalforn bay, on the northern side of the island of Gozo, lay jammed between two hills and the open sea.
Old maps depicted a narrower bay with its eastern coast straighter and its western tip protruding further north. Old photographs showed a little hamlet with a small, vigilant church surrounded by a handful of buildings. Both bays no longer existed. In the past forty years Marsalforn bay had turned into a thriving summer destination with promenades, restaurants and a large modern hotel. Only the port which the locals called *Menqa*, meaning 'little harbour', had remained simple and homely as in the old days.

Twenty-one year old Sarah lived alone on the eastern side of the bay, in a little house that overlooked the port. She had been living there for less than a year and was yet to get used to the whistling wind blowing between the crevices and howling through the empty courtyards.
Since her early childhood, she had always been afraid of thunderstorms, so, when in the early morning of that October day a thunderclap had woke her up, she had wrapped herself in blankets and had looked outside the window.
Torn between angst and fascination, she had watched the raging sea for a long while, then observing the fishermen return to the port she had picked up one of the white drawing boards piled up in a corner of the

room and, chalk in hand, she had started sketching the long lines of the bay, brushing with her fingertips the billowing clouds and waves. With delicate strokes, she had marked the port walls and lost herself in the details of the little boats chased by the waves.

Sarah had fallen in love with painting after moving to Gozo.

At first, the island had been her hideout, a place of escape from everyone and everything. Escaping from her native England she had found refuge in her grandmother's island, a place so different from the one where she had grown up that it felt just perfect for her wounded soul.

For the first year, she had lived in the little village of Munxar, on the south side of the island, living off the money she had earnt as a teacher abroad and taking life at an easy pace.

Every evening, at sunset, she had taken a walk to the nearby cliffs of Ta' Ċenċ and admired the beauty of the honeycombed coast in its solitary vastness and melancholic tones.

One evening, as she had sat on a stone watching a small boat coasting the overhanging cliffs, she had suddenly felt a presence behind her. Turning around she found an old man standing a few metres away, looking in her direction with fascinated eyes. Before him, perched on an old wooden easel, was a canvas on which his hand moved slowly in gentle movements, barely brushing the cloth.
Was he painting her portrait?
Feeling uneasy, Sarah had moved to stand up.

"Please, don't go," had said the man, "it will take just a few more minutes."
His voice was the voice of a man who had smoked too many cigarettes, yet his tone was gentle.
"Are you painting me?" Sarah had asked feeling shy.
"I am painting the view," he had replied without looking up from the canvas, "and you are part of it."
"Can I see it? I mean, when you're finished."
"Sure you can, but first," he made a pause, "first I'll need you to remain still."

When a few minutes later, Sarah had seen the painting, it had been something different from what she had expected. Every line on the canvas was sketched so coarsely that she had to move one step back to be able to recognise the cliffs diving into the sea. There was no trace of the orange sunset that coloured the horizon or of the clear sky that towered above them. In the upper part of the painting, a sombre cluster of dark clouds dominated the scene, bringing an oppressive feeling to the whole painting. Nonetheless, she liked it; there was so much energy in those cliffs overshadowed by the grey clouds that Sarah felt as if the old man had managed to look in her very soul and had somehow transposed it onto the canvas.

"You're a painter?" she had asked.
"Not exactly," he had said smiling, "let's say I normally paint using words."
"You mean you're a writer?"
The man nodded. He then put away the canvas and put it inside his bag.
Looking at the open sack Sarah noticed a bunch of pages tied up with a string.
"Is that the book you are working on?" she had asked pointing at the bag.
"You are one curious lady," he had replied looking at her.

She had smiled and for a moment they both looked at the sea.

"What's your name?" asked Sarah.
"Most people call me Sam."

Not too long later Sarah had decided to paint the same scene herself.
The first sketch, a blue ballpoint drawing outlined on an exercise book, had pleased her. So she had started painting, first with chalk, then with watercolours and oil paints.

Standing by her bedroom window, watching the storm batter the bay, Sarah tried to capture on canvas the power of the grey, menacing clouds and the white dashes of water that splashed against the blue surface of the sea.

As she painted, it never occurred to her that some boats were still trapped out at sea. So when she saw the shape of a small *luzzu* approaching the bay, she stopped painting for a moment and moved closer to the window.

Karmenu could not have seen the young foreign woman painting his boat from her bedroom window. When the *Ħamra* finally reached the port Karmenu found no one waiting for him. The thick rain had engulfed the bay and his brother's boat was not there.

CHAPTER 06

HOPE.

September 1954

On Ġorġ's twenty-second birthday, the boat he had been building for the previous five years was almost finished. He had fitted the engine, had sealed the planks and had started applying the second coat of blue paint. However, with just a few weeks away from its launch, Ġorġ had not yet found an appropriate name for his boat.
As tradition dictated, he had considered naming her Lola, *after his mother, but another boat had already the same name and Ġorġ had no intention of adding a number after the name.*

The inspiration came, as Ġorġ *liked to say, on a day of light.*

One September evening, as the sun approached the hills across Marsalforn bay, a ray of light made its way through the shed where Ġorġ had been working on the boat. Dazzled by the sudden gleam of light, Ġorġ had stopped working for a moment in order to admire the sun's reflection dashing on the boat's hull. His eyes gazed at the orange and grey shadows following the dark shape that projected on the wall.
Then, watching the rugged surface, his attention was caught by a little paper, which gleamed in the exact spot where the sun tinted the wall.

Under the thick wooden shelf full of dusty nets, creels, and empty bottles, hanging in what was normally a very dark part of the wall, was a small photograph.
Ġorġ pulled the image out of its hiding place and brought it outside, where the light was stronger.
It was an old photograph with a ridged white border and a large scratch on its top. It pictured a young man standing before a dgħajsa, *an old Gozitan sailing boat.*
It was a photograph that Ġorġ had never seen before, yet he had no doubt who the youth portrayed in the picture was. His square face and large frame left him with no doubts. It was an early picture of his father.
He looked younger than in any picture he had ever seen before, and elegant as he'd rarely ever seen him. He wore long, dark trousers, a vest and an elegant hat. His face was clean, with no trace of the large moustache or of the thick glasses he had worn in his later life. His eyes were proud and sincere, and stared straight into the camera with the joy of an athlete on the top podium.

Ġorġ smiled. In the seven years that had passed since his father's death, it was the first time he had smiled at his memory.

Holding the photograph by the kerosene lamp, he studied his father's features a little longer, then his attention switched to the boat in the background. It was an old sailing boat of a kind that was no longer in use on the island, with a tall mast and tapered prow. Written in capital letters on the side of the boat's prow was the name, "Latina"*.*

Ġorġ smiled again. He had found a name for his boat.

Nine years later at the time of death of his young wife, Ġorġ renamed the boat *Anna Marija.*

11th October 1980

Abandoned by her engine and at the mercy of the waves, the *Anna Marija* wavered at every quirk of the sea. On board the tottering boat, Ġorġ prayed to the *Virgin of Ta' Pinu* for the boat not to capsize.

"Mother of God, save our lives and spare the *Anna Marija*," he murmured bowing his head.

As his father prayed, Dwardu watched the incoming waves, searching for any vessel or sign of land.
All their attempts to revive the engine or to free the boat's screw had been unsuccessful and their only hope was now for someone to come and rescue them.

Time drifted away and evening advanced.

Like prisoners awaiting their sentence Ġorġ and Dwardu waited for the storm to end, for someone to find them or for the boat to capsize.

"Let's row," said Dwardu eventually, "I think I might have seen land," he continued, pointing in the distance. Yet his words bore no conviction.

So they rowed, hanging to a thread of hope.
But their desperate attempt was short lived.

"We are going nowhere," said Ġorġ after just a few minutes. The waves and currents were too strong and both of them were already exhausted.
The long day was taking its toll.

For some time they remained silent, sharing a piece of bread and listening to the drumming sound of the rain. Then came a small miracle. For just a moment, a short moment, the leaden clouds breached, the rain eased off and the horizon cleared, brightening like a lampshade on a grey wall.

Father and son eagerly scanned the horizon, looking for land, for a boat, or for a sign.

"There!" said Ġorġ suddenly, pointing his finger at an indistinct section of the sea.
"There," he said again, with his arm frozen mid-air.

Dwardu followed his father's gaze and his finger but saw nothing.
"Do you see it?" asked his father, with a voice that could barely contain his emotion. "About a few hundred meters from here; just there; it's a float. A yellow float."
He smiled, with his lips stretched open, one of those rare smiles that defeated his thick beard.
Then fishing for the oars he said: "Let's row."

CHAPTER 07

MEMORIES.

Ġorġ and Dwardu rowed ceaselessly, fighting against each wave and pushing through their limits.
Almost an hour later, they reached the yellow buoy. They tied the *Anna Marija* to the float's rope and drank from one of the two remaining bottles of water. Then, exhausted, they rested.

It was late when they caught their breath. The wind had abated and the layer of dark clouds had slowly blended with the black tinge of the night. Yet, the storm was not over. The rain still pelted over their heads and the lightning still brightened each corner of the horizon.

Lying under the tarpaulin, they rested close to each other, thoughtfully waiting.

"We'll have to buy a second engine," said Ġorġ looking away into the storm.
They had been through this issue many times before.
"Pawlu *tal-Sellum* has one for sale," said Dwardu, "he wants forty Liri for it, but I am sure he'll sell it for half that price."
"Maybe it might be time to buy a new boat."

Dwardu could not help noticing the tinge of sadness that had pervaded his father's voice.

They had discussed that too, many times before, but to Ġorġ, the boat bearing the name of his late wife meant more than it did to his son who had barely any memory of his mother.

Dwardu's few memories of his mother had nothing to do with the boat that bore her name. He had been just four years old when she had died.

January 1963.

Anna Marija had died in January, when the hills were green and the winds strong.

Waking up the following morning, still unaware of his mother's death, four-year-old Dwardu had waited for her to wake him up. Tucked under the grey covers of his wooden bed, with his eyes closed and his arms lying by the side of his body, he had pretended to be asleep.
With a smile of anticipation, he had silently listened to the clatter of the cutlery coming from the kitchen and, once the clatter had ended, had expected his mother's steps to reach him through the corridor.
When instead, he had heard the kitchen chair creak under the weight of a sitting body, he had decided to change his plan.
Leaving his brown, worn out teddy bear sleeping in a small cot beside his bed, he had tiptoed through the corridor and had prepared to surprise his mother with a loud cry.
There was an eerie silence oozing throughout the house.

Dwardu realised something was wrong when, entering the kitchen, instead of his mother, he found Nanna Lola.
Nanna Lola sat on the same wooden chair his father always sat on, leaning on the table as if she was about to fall asleep. Then, her eyes had suddenly turned towards him, making him shiver.
It was her eyes. They were red and tired. But as soon as Dwardu looked into her big frame glasses, her expression changed into something more relaxed.
"Where is mum?" Dwardu had asked.
For a moment, the question lingered in the air, then dispersed in the bottle of milk and the empty glass that Nanna Lola was placing on the table.
"Have some milk."
Pouring the milk with care, Nanna Lola smiled.

But her smile was not a real smile but a lie painted over her lips.

"Where is mummy?" Dwardu had asked again.
Nanna Lola had not resisted a second time, her wrinkled face had crumpled, her glasses had slightly lifted above her nose and she had broken in tears.
"She went to Malta," she ventured between sobs.

Watching Nanna Lola cry, Dwardu felt uncertain whether to console her or not. He had never seen an adult cry, and Nanna Lola was much more than an adult, she was an old woman.
Was a child supposed to comfort a crying adult? Yes, he thought. And, still not knowing what his grandmother was crying about, Dwardu had reached for her arm and with his most compassionate tone told her.
"Don't cry nanna. Mum will be back soon," he said.

Two hours later, the truth had arrived.

“Mum is not coming back!” said aunt Philomena before adding that his mother loved him and that God himself, had asked her to join his angels.

“We don’t need a new boat,” said Dwardu to his father, “a second engine will be enough.”

Then a new lightning crossed the sky. As they glimpsed the view, both men’s expression changed.

“You saw it too?” asked Dwardu in a tone of disbelief.
“*Iva*” confirmed his father in Maltese.

Framed between the waves and the clouds, the lash of light had revealed the dark shape of their island. Gozo, its silhouette barely bigger than a mole on the sea’s skin. Yet it was there.

CHAPTER 08

GUILT.

The night had arrived furtively, the shadows had grown dimmer and the bay had turned its lights on.
By nine o'clock in the evening, the news that the *Anna Marija* had not yet returned to land had spread and a small group of fishermen had gathered by the port.

The rain had ceased but the thunderstorm was still raging in the distance.

Away from the group, standing by the side of the port, Karmenu searched the sea. With the darkness, the chances of seeing the boat coming back had become slimmer.

"Why are they not back yet?" wondered Karmenu, knowing something had obviously gone wrong.
In his worst fears he imagined the *'Anna Marija'* overwhelmed by the waves, and Ġorġ and Dwardu gasping to keep afloat while the sea battered and pushed them beneath its surface.

It was his fault, he thought. He should not have returned to the port leaving them at sea. He had deserted them.

His heart clenched and he wished he had remained with them.
But he had not, and all he could do now was to go back out to sea and search for them. But the fear of going out

to sea and not finding them frightened him even more than the long wait.
What if they were dead, he thought, and soon the thought of another death entered his mind.

"Anna Marija" he whispered.
Fighting against tears, he tried to push the thought away, but it wouldn't go.
Yet it was the thought of his brother's wife that helped him make his mind up.

"I am going out to look for them," he said to himself trying to sound braver than he really felt.

Two young fishermen helped him to lower the *Ħamra* in the water, but none of them joined him aboard.

Karmenu rolled up the tarpaulin, moved to the engine, then glanced up at the docks.
Looking at him, curved as a tailor, was *Fanal.*
"I am coming with you," said the old man.

For an instant, Karmenu thought of ignoring the old man, pretending he hadn't heard him, but decided against it. Three eyes were surely better than one, he thought.

The old man boarded the boat and sat on the middle thwart; he buttoned up his jacket and covered himself with one of Karmenu's old rugged jumpers, which he found beneath the tarpaulin.

"Where did you see your brother last?" asked *Fanal* as soon as the boat had gone out of the port.
"North of Gozo, maybe ten miles off the coast." replied Karmenu.

"Ten miles? What the hell were you doing so far from the coast in a storm like this? Where you trying to reach Tunisia?" grunted the old man.

Regretting having allowed the man onboard, Karmenu gave no explanation; instead he focused on the mouth of the bay and made himself deaf to the man's grumbling. The boat danced over the choppy sea and the two men bent against the gusts of the chilling wind facing the sea.

"What took you so long?" growled the old man as the boat was out of the bay. "By now, the waves might have pushed them as far as Africa. Your brother would have come out long before had it been you out there at sea. He would not have waited for the day to be over. He would have gone out in the afternoon when he still had a chance of finding you alive."

"I saw fishermen praying today; going through each decade of the rosary beads, babbling prayers one after the other. How brave. Two men are lost at sea and all the fellow fishermen can do is pray. What for, I ask myself. Has God ever listened to them? Go out, I say. Show you are men. Show there is a little bit of Roman blood still left on this island."

Karmenu listened without saying anything. The old man was right, he thought with regret. Nobody had had the courage to face the storm, but he was wrong on one point. His brother would not have gone out with the boat in the afternoon. Ġorġ would not have returned to the port in the first place, not without him.

Of the two of them, Ġorġ had always been the stronger and the braver. Karmenu had always assumed that had it not been for his partial blindness he would have been like his brother, yet the accident that had left Karmenu blind in the left eye had shaped his character much less than his father's attitude towards him.

Physically, the two brothers looked very much alike. Both of them had a slight build, their skin was dark and their nose pronounced.
The most obvious difference between their faces was Karmenu's mangled left eye, and more recently, Ġorġ's beard, which he had grown wild since Anna Marija's death. It was a sign of mourning, he said.
Karmenu too, sometimes, felt like growing a beard for the same reason, but his mourning wasn't public and eventually he always shaved his beard off.

At a superficial glance, the two brothers appeared similar even in character, both were calm and silent, religious and simple. However a deeper look revealed significant differences. As much as Ġorġ was confident, Karmenu's was hesitant and weak.

Eventually Karmenu passed the torch to *Fanal* and asked him to start searching the sea. The old man took it in his hands with unexpected strength and started shifting it towards every corner of the horizon.
But the light was not strong enough.
"Maybe they'll see the light," said Karmenu defensively.

Fanal shook his head.
"Dead people don't see lights!" he said. "You know that if they are dead, you will have them on your conscience, you more than anyone."
Then a lightning struck a distant corner of the horizon.

CHAPTER 09

FIRE, WATER, AIR.

Dwardu felt the lightning arrive. Light and sound arrived simultaneously, with the blast being loud as a firearm shot at point-blank range.
The boat shook and Dwardu felt the air sucked out of his lungs, his skin creased, his eyes bulged, then his body went limp.
Blackness replaced light as silence followed the rumble, then arrived numbness, then oblivion.

Dwardu never realised he had fallen into the water. But soon it was just water, waves and darkness again. More darkness than Dwardu had ever imagined in his life; blackness that entered deep inside him leaving him cold and paralysed.

Lost in limbo, with his mind still stolen by the blast, he swam and fought against the waves.

The sound of the darkness and the constant deep rumble murmured nightmares into Dwardu's ears. Then a thunder exploded, loud and near by.
This time he saw no light, just sound: a roar, low and resonant. The air shook again, and more waves battered his face.

Frightened and wet, he trembled.

The wind whistled and the rain crushed on the sea surface. Dwardu gasped for air as the waves brought him down. He felt the boat slipping away and in the desperate and subconscious attempt to reach for the vessel, his hands frantically stretched all around but found only water, air, and blackness. Every inch of his world was now filled with water which gripped him with its million tentacles, pulling him down to its depths.

As unconsciousness drew closer, in a last desperate attempt to survive, Dwardu gasped.
Air. He longed for air. A breath, he thought, just a small one.
He remembered keeping his breath under water, in summer when he was young and he jumped off the rock of *Għar Qawqla* clinging to the sea bottom like a crab or a sea urchin. Air, he thought again, then his thoughts started blurring.

There are five phases in drowning, he had read somewhere.
The first phase is prolonged submersion which gives way to an exhausting struggle for air. The body tenaciously holds its breath until the carbon dioxide is so high that the brain gives order to inhale anyway. This gulping of water is followed by coughing and vomiting which leads to the loss of consciousness. Convulsions come next, followed by involuntary respiratory movements that culminate mostly in heart failure. After that, death occurs within two or three minutes.

He was in phase three, thought Dwardu, holding his breath tenaciously.

Air. He wrenched, searching the water. Then, the first memories started flooding his thoughts.

In his mind, there was his younger self, riding his first bicycle down a hill in Marsalforn, falling and scarring himself on the stony path; there was his mother, leaning over him and screaming at the sight of the chameleon he had hidden next to her pillow. Then, there was his father, at first calm then angry, shouting at him for something he had done wrong. What, he could not remember. Finally there was the sobbing of *Nanna Lola* the morning after his mother's death.

Many more thoughts ran through his mind but all of them vanished the moment his senses felt the temperature of the water around him change. Dwardu felt warm, like the warmth one feels on a winter day when the sun emerges unexpectedly from the clouded sky. It was his unconscious part that first realised that the warmth he was feeling was due to the contact of his body with the air above the sea surface. Before his mind could even grasp the notion, he had already started gasping for that air he so longed for. At the limit of his endurance, rushed by man's most primal need, Dwardu's mouth opened in search of oxygen. As the air reached his lungs, Dwardu felt a moment of dizziness, then a faint smile crisped his lips.

He had inhaled just a tiny portion of his lungs' capacity when another wave had reached him and taken him down. The sea mixed with the air, and Dwardu felt the wetness of the water and the taste of the salt flooding his mouth and his nostrils. He coughed. As the wave kept pulling him down, Dwardu tried to clamber up the invisible rope of hope that hung from the air. He tried to swim, pushing with all his strength against the sudden tide but the force of the waves overpowered him. He felt his senses die and a thin line inside him break, then, when he felt completely lost, something hard hit his face. It was like being hit by the board of a swing. His face flushed and a new ray of hope cut through his consciousness. With his arms stretched, he reached for the hard object, trying to grab hold of it, then numbness embraced him, and another wave pulled him down.

CHAPTER 10

WAVES.

Dwardu could not remember hoisting himself back aboard the *Anna Marija*, but the water was gone, replaced by the comforting hardness of the boat's wooden boards. The violent brightness of the lightning had left him temporarily blind and the strenuous fight against the waves had taken away all of his strength. More thunder overwhelmed his mind while the rain and fever battered his body. For countless minutes, abandoned on the bottom boards of the boat, Dwardu lay unconscious.
Spasms rattled his body.

Many times, Dwardu awoke and dived back into unconsciousness. Deep, uncontrolled thoughts rattled his mind; images poured down his eyes like flashlights through the dark.
He imagined an old man looking at him, sitting cross-legged on a sandy beach, smoking a pipe and staring quietly at his inert body.

Time passed slowly but the man didn't move.
Dwardu felt the tides flutter his body and the sun crease his forehead; he sensed the sand drift beneath his back and the wind ruffle his hair.

Was he God?

"Are you God?" asked Dwardu barely moving his lips.
The old man looked at him and smiling shook his head.

"No, I am not."
His white hair waved in the wind and settled over his shoulders.

"Who are you then?" asked Dwardu.
This time the man didn't answer immediately. He drew on his pipe and stared at the sea.
"I am you," he said eventually, "or better, it's you who is me" and slowly puffed out the smoke into the air.

CHAPTER 11

BACK.

When *Fanal* and Karmenu returned to the island, the bay was dark and the little row of houses that rimmed the coast was silently asleep.
Their desperate attempt to find the *Anna Marija* in the middle of the night had been fruitless. The sea was too vast and their boat too small.

Five hours later, they were back where they had started.

Overwhelmed by the long night, on the way back to the island, *Fanal* had fallen asleep; his shoulders curved under the thick woollen cover, his body softened and his head slumped onto his chest.
Karmenu looked at the old man dozing off and smiled.
In spite of the strong words *Fanal* had thrown at him, he had appreciated the old man's help, his passion for life and his combative spirit; all qualities that he missed.
His presence had reminded him of the time when he and Ġorġ had been fishing together, before Dwardu's teenage years, before the *Ħamra* and before Anna Marija's death. Times he often missed.

As they entered the port, nobody was waiting for them; all the lights were off and the car park was empty. As Karmenu glanced at his house, he was surprised to find the lights off too. He looked around in the hope of seeing the *Anna Marija* safely moored in the port, but she wasn't there.

"We're back." said Karmenu grabbing the mooring rope. *Fanal*'s shoulders and head straightened, then he turned towards Karmenu and looked him in the eyes.
"We will find them tomorrow with the light." He said calmly.

CHAPTER 12

CONSCIOUSNESS.

It was early morning when Dwardu regained consciousness. At first, with his eyes still closed, he struggled to understand where he was. He felt the soft waving of the boat and heard the rhythmical swishing of the water hitting the bow, but remembered nothing of the storm.
As he moved, his body ached. His head felt like a heavy stone and his arms like tree branches.
Had he been drinking? he asked himself.

Reality reached him a moment later as the sound of the waves gave way to his consciousness and a sudden feeling of apprehension crawled up his chest.
Opening his eyes, he recognised the bottom boards of the *Anna Marija*; the gentle rocking of the boat he knew as waves and the first memories of the lightning leapt back to his mind.

With his eyes still weak, Dwardu tried to lift himself up. He pushed onto his right arm, pressing with his hand against the wet wooden boards of the boat.

As he managed to lift himself a few inches from the floor, a faint shriek escaped through his lips, then his body collapsed, face first.
The strong twinge of pain that crossed the right side of his body made him scream, then a feeling of numbness

seized his right arm bringing a tingling sensation which spread throughout his body.

He was blacking out again.

Embracing the numbness, Dwardu let himself go.
He relaxed every muscle of his body and waited for the blackness to relieve his pain. Then, as the dizziness was about to engulf him, while his body prickled and his eyes rolled back, Dwardu thought of his father.
Where is he? he asked himself. And the need for an answer made unconsciousness recede.

"Father!" he whispered; salt and wind squandered his voice.
I need water, he thought, just a sip, maybe, two. And swallowing hard, he remembered the bottle he and his father had been drinking from.

As his arms searched for new strength, he felt the wetness of the boat's bottom boards and sensed the damp liquid sticking to his body.

Blood.

"I am bleeding to death", he mumbled to himself and, as to prove himself right, he suddenly noticed the painful feeling that throbbed at the back of his head. A low, thundering heartbeat, constant and hypnotic.

Again he thought of his father. Where was he? Was he aboard the boat?
"Father" he called one more time.
There was fear in his voice.

Waiting for his father's voice to reach his ears, Dwardu studied each sound: the light creaking of the prow, the rolling of one of the plastic bottles and the rustling of water.

Suddenly he was fully awake, aware of many more sounds and of other parts of his body that throbbed and ached: his back, his right shoulder, his stomach, his nose.
He smiled. That little orchestra of various pains meant one significant thing: he was alive, wounded but alive.

This new awareness raised his consciousness and brought back his memory. He could remember.
The storm, the engine, the sideboard, the yellow buoy, the lightning, the sea, the boat.
He remembered it all, he thought, and as each memory surfaced, still-images danced before his eyes.
He remembered the old man he had dreamed of and the struggle to get back onto the boat.

“Father, are you there?” he called for a third time, this time as loud as he could.
Again, there was no answer.

Maybe he was lying at the front of the boat unconscious, bleeding to death, as he was.
He had to look for him.

Again, the throbbing at the back of his head stifled his thoughts.

Careful not to move the right part of his body, Dwardu slowly shifted his left hand from under his chest and reached for the aching part at the rear of his head.
His fingers ran through his hair, then found a wound.
It was, dense and clotted. Dry blood. He was no longer bleeding.

As he opened his eyes, the pain intensified; the light darted past his eyelids thumping his head.
Slowly the pounding lessened and he was able to see.

He felt weak though; his eyelids pleaded to be closed; his vision blurred. But he could see. And what he saw was a red liquid lapping over his face.
It was too thin to be just blood. It had to be mixed with water.

For the first time since he had regained consciousness, Dwardu realised exactly where he was. He was at the stern's end of the boat, between the engine and the rear thwart, next to one of the nets. Then, turning his head to the right, he saw the sky. The dark clouds were gone, the rain had stopped and the sun was high.

Putting the pain aside, he decided to try to lift himself up again. This time he leant on his left elbow, and pushed with all his strength.

It took a few minutes. But he eventually managed to lift himself up and sprawl against the bundled fishing net.

His father was not on the boat. With the light still piercing like needles into his eyes, he nervously looked at each corner of the boat.
Inside the boat, the blood mixed with sea water rippled after each wave.

Pulling himself onto the middle thwart of the boat, he found the bottle of water. He drank avidly, washing away the taste of salt that permeated his mouth. Then, again, he looked for his father, this time widening his search to the sea.
He saw the yellow buoy and the rope that fastened the boat to it, but nothing else.

The sea was calm; in the distance the colours pink, orange and red piled up on each other leaning on top of the straight blue line of the horizon. Next to them, tinged in blue, was his island: Gozo.

It was there, where it had always been, the same as he had seen it every morning of his life.

As the sands of time shifted through the glass, Dwardu watched the morning become day while scanning the sea.
Once or twice, he saw far away boats, distant and frail. But as fast as they appeared, they disappeared.

More uneventful hours passed. The sun reached its summit and the wind decreased.

"Somebody will come!" he said to himself drinking the last sip of water.

PART II - Water

CHAPTER 13

THE CLUB.

The villagers of Nadur have always called it 'the Club'; yet besides a few newspaper-cuttings taped to the wall and an old silver cup on display on one of the shelves, the Club is little more than a bar, small and dusty, with a row of wooden tables and two benches connecting them all.

It's a place stuck in the past, where everything seems outdated, from the colourful portrait of Jesus to the ageing bottles of Scotch whisky and the black and white photograph of a football team that no longer exists.
But it's not just the fittings that make the Club seem old. Its entrance is low; barely six feet tall, and so narrow that from the street it looks like a wardrobe, with its door screened by a nylon curtain, thin enough to trap flies and people alike.
The lamps are aligned like skittles and the walls, once white, are now grey from smoke and dust.

For as long as I can remember, the Club has been my favourite bar; its dim, cool air makes it a prime choice for summer whilst its cosiness suits the winter to perfection.
I like its quietness and the unpretentious mood that makes days pass so anonymously that each one resembles the previous.

On the thirteenth of October, I was sitting in a corner of the Club, reading one of the local newspapers and drinking a coffee, when the kappillan appeared at the bar's entrance wrapped in a black mantel.

The priest nodded and I replied closing my eyes, more for politeness than for any Catholic belief.

It was almost four o'clock. The morning had passed in a thunderstorm and the afternoon looked to promise more rain.
Besides the barman, old Ġużepp, and myself the Club was deserted. Ronny, the village grocer, had left the bar to open his own shop and the barber who usually popped by during his afternoon break, was at home sick.

"Bonġu Ġorġ" said the kappillan moving past the fly net and into the bar. The barman nodded back to the priest, then went back to cleaning the glasses.
It was his wife who greeted the priest for everyone else.
"'Morning Dun Karist." she shouted leaning out of the little window that connected the kitchen to the bar. "What terrible weather!"

The kappillan sat by the counter and the barman placed a steaming glass of black tea before him.

Outside it had started raining again, and the sound of water trickling through the pipes of the courtyard could be heard through the closed windows.

At four o'clock the barkeeper turned up the volume of the radio to listen to the news. As he did so, every other sound in the bar seemed to cease.

After the latest political debate, the news that everyone had been waiting for arrived.

"... while one of the two vessels that went missing at sea yesterday has safely returned to its port, one boat with two Gozitan fishermen onboard has not yet been located. The small luzzu, which ventured out to sea before Saturday's storm, was last seen more than twenty-four hours ago. The

Maritime Authority believes the vessel has most probably been pushed to the East by the prevailing winds and are concentrating their search in the area.
Their spokesman, Mark Ellul ..."

"... we are doing everything we can. All available patrol boats and rescue aircraft have been deployed. We have asked for assistance to the Italian Navy and alerted the Tunisian authorities ..."

That's how I learnt of the missing boat.

CHAPTER 14

RESCUE.

At first, it was just a white dot on the most distant part of the horizon. Dwardu's eyes blinked, then he looked again.

A few minutes later, Dwardu saw it again: a tiny bright point, as big as a speck of sand fluttering against the dark blue surface of the water.
A boat. He couldn't say if big or small, but it was definitely a boat.

Gradually, the speck of sand grew into a grain of salt and Dwardu decided it was moving in his direction. Galvanised, he looked around inside the *Anna Marija*, moved some of the ropes, and untied one of the jute sacks that enveloped the nets.
Next, he stood in the centre of the boat and, trying to overcome his pain, he started waving the boathook with the sack attached to its extremity, but the pain was too intense and the vessel still too far.
So he waited as the grain became a seed, then a pebble, and finally a boat.

But it wasn't until the boat was just a few yards away that Dwardu recognised the man aboard. His image was still very clear in his mind. He was the man from his dream; the man with the pipe that had been leaning over him on the deserted beach.

For a moment everything stopped. The boat stopped advancing, the wind stopped blowing and the sea flattened.

Was the boat a dream?

But just when he expected the boat to disappear, the old man waved.

"Are you fine?" called the old man.
It was a voice that felt real and Dwardu decided to believe in it.
"I am all right," he lied, feeling the throbbing increase with his words.

That was all. There were no more words; no questions about his father, no enquiry about the lightning and no mention of the engine's status. Or, if there ever were any words, Dwardu could not remember any.
Once the boat was close enough for the two vessels to almost touch, the old man threw a rope, which Dwardu tied to the stern, freeing the yellow buoy.

Rescue was a simple as that.

Whisked by a light breeze, the two boats advanced through a gentle sea, hand in hand, like sisters.

Eventually, it was Dwardu who spoke.
"Has my father been found?" he shouted over the trotting sound of the engine.
On the other boat, the man turned around. His beard neatly trimmed and his jacket clean and new.
He cupped his hand around his ear to indicate Dwardu should repeat the question. He then shook his head and over the wind he shouted "I don't know."

Dwardu didn't ask further questions. His thoughts took over. 'I don't know' meant that most probably, his father was still out there, in the water maybe dead or maybe dying. His silence meant that he was abandoning him; leaving him to die without even trying to rescue him.
But he felt too tired to think further.
He looked at the sea and left his mind flood with thoughts that had no flow.

When they were in sight of the port the man turned around.

"We're almost there!" he said smiling.
Dwardu nodded, feeling strange at the prospect of being back without his father.

"What's your name?" he shouted next.
"My name is Samuel," replied the man from the other boat.

CHAPTER 15

ANNA MARIJA.

November 1962.

Nineteen-sixty-two had been a year of extremes. January had set the lowest temperatures ever recorded on the Maltese Islands, bringing the first snow anyone could remember. Snowflakes had descended slowly through the sky melting into rain before touching the ground.
A few months later the snow had been forgotten, replaced by an intense heat. After a series of short heat spells, July had brought temperatures of over forty degrees; the reservoirs had gone dry and so had the land.

1962 was also to be the last year Anna Marija would live in its entirety. Yet, besides the unlikely snow of January and the extreme heat of July, her year passed with little or no remarkable events.
Her diary showed only a few entries.

On the 16th of April, the day she had turned 26, she had written, "I spoke to dad today, he wished me happy birthday and then we talked of the usual things. It felt so normal that I can hardly believe we haven't spoken to each other for over six months".

On June 14th she had written about refusing a teaching post for the following year, then there were no entries until November.

Since she had married almost five years earlier, Anna Marija had stopped recording all her thoughts and emotions on paper. Once, she had disclosed to her diary even her most private emotions; the ones she hadn't dared confess to the priest or to her sisters.
Once, she had described the kiss her cousin Victor had given her returning from the beach, and another time she had confessed her love for an English soldier met at the village feast.

It was no longer that way.

Her last entry for 1962 was dated 18th of November.
It was not a sentence but a photograph with a pen-drawn frame around it. Beneath it were the words: "Dwardu and me".

Next to it was the torn edge of a missing page.

After a week of clear sky, the weather had turned grey and the northern winds had brought the first taste of the coming winter.

Ġorġ had gone to the main island to pick up a new inboard engine bought the previous week. He was going to be out all day, as in those days a trip to Malta was a long journey, tedious on land and dangerous at sea.
Anna Marija had woken up in the early morning with Ġorġ and had then returned to bed. Once there, she had tried to sleep, but could not. Her eyes didn't close and her mind kept thinking. The ceiling, she noticed, had a little crack by the side of the wall; a small, almost imperceptible mark that followed the corner of the room and ended just before the large metal beam.
She had to speak to Ġorġ, she thought.

She should have spoken to him over breakfast, but had not done so.

She got up. She liked it when the house was silent; when the only sounds she could hear were the ones coming from the port; muffled and distant. When the ticking of the kitchen clock echoed gently and when the morning light pressed smoothly against the windows.

Opening the middle drawer of the kitchen dresser, she reached with her hand under two old tablecloths, and found her diary, wrapped in a white handkerchief.

"I am pregnant, again", *she wrote in the middle of the page.*
The previous evening the doctor had confirmed what she had already known for many weeks.

Then she went on writing.

"When I was a young girl I wanted to be a writer or a poet.
As a child, my elder sister read me fairy tales about castles and beautiful princesses. Then I grew, and fascinated by the world of words, I wrote in my diary, invented stories, confessed my thoughts and dreamt about places that I had never seen.
As my body began flourishing, I started reading Jane Austen, Dylan Thomas and Emily Brontë. Their words were so full of emotion that I read them over and over.
Then I fell in love. But my love was not to be. So, I stopped reading and I wrote. Page after page my diaries filled up with words, but my heart still felt empty.

I started teaching and reading Enid Blyton and Beatrix Potter to my pupils.
Then, one day as I was walking along the narrow alleys of my life, I saw the cobbled streets beneath my feet transform into a dirt path. It was a nice path, bordered on both sides by low rubble walls, behind which stretched the countryside, green and lush. I had no choice, I told myself, and followed the path.
At the end of the path, I found the sea, with its seductive beauty. It was a windy day but the sea was calm, so I sat down and observed the neat line that separated the world of the birds from that of fish.
I didn't know, but my life was about to change again.
That evening, I met a fisherman and as soon as I met him, my heart was already beating for him.
He was nice, shy, quiet and I was young and full of life.
The following day I started reading D. H. Laurence and Hermann Hesse.
My father said: "Not with a fisherman" but my life was already his. Besides, how could a carpenter accuse a fisherman of being simple?
Not long after the wedding came the first child and soon I was reading children's stories again.
Sometimes I wrote, briefly, using my imagination more than my emotions.
One evening, before going to bed, I told my husband I would read him a poem I had written. And though it might not have been the most beautiful poem, it was the best I had ever written so far.

It started with the words "These gentle hills" ... and it talked about my island, about my body and about my desire for life.
As I read my poem, my husband listened. His eyes fixed, kind and patient.
But though his head was nodding at each sentence, I could see that none of my words were reaching him through his armour of uncomplicated thoughts.
That night I did not sleep. At times, I cried, silently, pressing my head into the pillow.
It was probably my fault. Had I written about the sea or about little coloured boats that dotted the port he would have possibly understood my words. But he had not and I felt defeated.
"I will never write again" I told myself.
So I started reading Camus and Salinger.
My son was now a young toddler and I dedicated my life to him.
But things changed again. Another person was knocking on my door."

Anna Marija re-read the last sentence then she gripped the page she had been writing, and tore it from the book.

She started crying.
How could words be more painful than thoughts?
Then her four-year-old son entered the room and Anna Marija quickly wiped the tears from her eyes and turned to face him, smiling.

For the rest of the morning, Anna Marija and her son went out for a walk around the bay.
The greyness of the previous evening had dispersed. Stretched by the wind, a small group of horizontal clouds

clawed the blue sky; beneath them, the sea was calm and the port was quiet and empty.

They sat by the little beach in the middle of the bay, Dwardu on the sand and Anna Marija on the small wall that separated the beach from the street.

"How would you like to have a little brother or sister?" Dwardu looked at his mother unsure of what to say, then replied in a thoughtful tone.
"Only if we call him Pietru." he said, looking thoughtful.
Anna Marija smiled. Pietru was her sister's son, a little boy just a few months older than Dwardu.
"Come here" she said extending her hand to her son. The boy looked at his mother with his eyes wide open then walked towards her.
They hugged. Then Anna Marija opened her bag and took out a brand new photographic camera. Her sister, who lived in Malta, had left it behind during her family visit.
"Let's take a nice picture." she said.

CHAPTER 16

TIC – TIC.

At the sight of the port and of the hotel that towered above it, Dwardu's heart shrank and his thoughts went back to his father. He pictured him sitting on the docks by the grey walls, his head low, his legs outstretched and his fingers weaving rapidly through a fishing net.
Then, the bay slowly embraced him. He was back home.

Entering the port, there were many familiar faces looking at him; muffled voices, shouts and prayers reached him from every direction.
With the innocence of a child, forgetting all that had happened to him, Dwardu smiled and waved in every direction. It was like coming back from war, he thought.
He waved to his grandmother, who was tucked beneath a large black veil, to Karmenu and to the many fishermen that had gathered on the docks.

As he had done hundreds of times before, he then moored the *Anna Marija* at the usual place.
The *Ħamra* was not there, he noticed. The only two boats in the water were the two green vessels owned by the Busuttil brothers.

With his body still in pain, he secured the mooring rope at the boat's stern and fitted the loose slipknot at the prow. He tied the knots around the props and stepped out of the boat onto firm land.

The moment his feet touched the solid ground of the island, all his forgotten thoughts seemed to reach him at once.
Had his father been found? He wondered, looking around the people, hands and voices that surrounded him.

"You made it back!" said the familiar voice of one of the fishermen. Then his legs started to soften, his knees buckled and his body gave up.

He saw feet: some bare, others in flip-flops or in sandals; a few wrapped in leather shoes, brown or black. He blacked out.

Tic - tic.
How many times had he lain still in his bed listening to the metallic ticking of the kitchen clock? It must have been thousands.
Sometimes he counted the seconds, just to know how many minutes it would take to fall asleep. It was a mesmerising sound, like the sound of a flag flapping in the wind or the steady pulse of blood throbbing in your head.

Yes, a steady pulse of blood throbbing in his head ... that's what it was.

"Can you hear me?" came a voice from above him.
It was the voice of Dr. Caruana, the retired doctor who lived in one of the oldest buildings in the bay.
"*Iva*, I can hear you," murmured Dwardu.

It was then that he realised he was laying in port in the shade of a docked vessel.

He was offered water and drank avidly. How good it tasted.

Then a new voice asked: “Where is your father?”
Right, where was his father?
It was the voice *spettur* Agius, the police inspector.

So, he had not been found, Dwardu thought.

“*Ma nafx*!” I don’t know! He replied.

“Was he not with you on the boat?”

“He was with me on the boat when the lightning hit us, but I haven’t see him since then.” he said.
He then tried to pull himself up but a hand pushed him back down. “Stay down” said the doctor “you have a nasty cut at the back of your head. You’d better not move too much.”

“You were hit by lightning?” asked *spettur* Agius.
Dwardu nodded. “It hit the boat,” he said.

The inspector moved away towards of the boat. “I’ll need a few men”, he shouted to the crowd with a tone of authority.

Dwardu followed the inspector’s movements with his eyes, then *Bebbuxu*, the neighbour’s son, blocked his view by kneeling before him.

Dwardu smiled on seeing the boy but felt the throbbing intensify.
The boy swung his head and smiled back lifting the right corner of his mouth as he always did. He was born that way: skinny, gnarled, a little loony and always smiling.

Dwardu looked at the crippled body of the boy and tried to look as if he was not in pain.

"How are you Christopher?" he said calling the boy by his proper name.

Bebbuxu didn't reply to the question but his smile widened, showing a row of uneven teeth.

"Are you taking me on the boat, Dwardu?" he asked instead.
A couple of years earlier, Dwardu had taken *Bebbuxu* on a short excursion on the *Anna Marija.* The boy had played with the water, giggled and generally enjoyed the trip so much that since that day. Dwardu had quickly become one of his best friends and he had done everything to stay worthy of such a title.
"Not today," replied Dwardu, "I'm sorry."

"Bring it up!" shouted the inspector, pointing to the *Anna Marija.* He then moved back next to Dwardu and said "*Jiddispjacini,* I am sorry, Dwardu, we have to seize the boat, it's the law."

CHAPTER 17

HAPPY BIRTHDAY KARMENU!

Three days had passed since the storm had hit the "*Anna Marija*" and neither Ġorġ nor his body had yet been found.

In the dim evening light, sitting in a hidden corner of the port, Karmenu waited for the last fishing boat to return from the sea. In the last few days, he had passed more time at sea than on land. He had searched each wave and had studied each crest. He had seen new storms form in the distance and disappear past the horizon.
Many times during those few days, he had seen growing gales whip up the waves. Often, he had prayed. With his eyes closed, he had whispered his thoughts to himself and shared them with the Lord. Twice, at the sight of some object in the midst of the sea, he had felt his hope rejuvenate only to dissolve away.
Now, watching the last boat returning sombrely to the port, he felt like grieving.

He had slept less than a handful of hours since the thunderstorm and now tiredness was catching up with his body. The bones of his neck hurt, his eyes felt like thick curtains ready to drop and his hands twitched ceaselessly rubbing knuckles and thumbs against one another. But his tiredness went deeper than his skin and bones. He felt like an empty shell left sweltering in the sun.

Leaving the port would have felt like an act of surrender; a desertion his brother did not deserve.
At home, he would have seen his old mother only to tell her, one more time, that Ġorġ, her firstborn son, had not yet been found, that he was still at sea, lost and alone.

He lit a cigarette and dragged on it deeply while looking at the port with his tired eyes.

"He is dead," he thought and a shiver walked down his spine.

"What are you doing there, crouching between the boats like a cat?" asked Ġorġ.
With his gaze fixed on the port Karmenu dragged onto the cigarette then closed both his eyes.
"What should I do?" he replied in a downcast tone.
"Come out and look for me," replied Ġorġ.
"I did. Everyone did, but no one can find you."
"So? That's it. You are ready to give up? How long will it take before you learn not to give up?"

Karmenu kept his eyes closed.
"I am scared," he said.
"Scared of what, Karm? There is nothing to be afraid of. Around me, there is just sea."
"I am scared of finding you dead, Ġorġ. Of remaining alone, one more time."
"There is Dwardu, Karm, you are not alone."
"I don't know about Dwardu, Ġorġ, he is your son, but he is nothing like you!"
"Then come and find me. Try it one more time." said Ġorġ's voice. "I am asking you Karm, don't leave me alone."
"But what if I don't find you?"
"Then I'll die."

"Jesus, Ġorġ, you make it sound as if it's all my fault."
"No Karm. It's not. But come fast, the water is cold. You know how cold it can be."
"I know."
He knew.

February 1942

On the 25th of the month, eight-year-old Karmenu was woken by his father. It was early in the morning and the sun had still not made its way through the fissures around the closed shutters.
"Karm, you are coming with me today" his father said, standing in the darkness in the middle of the room.
Karmenu jumped out of bed and dressed rapidly. If there was something he had learned in his short existence, it was not to make his father angry.
In his eyes, his father was not only big and bad tempered but he also hated children.
In reality, Raymond Muscat, Ġorġ and Karmenu's father, neither hated children nor was he a giant. He was a medium-built man of average height with a dense moustache growing over his lips and thick glasses that framed his eyes in many concentric circles. He had a large head, which was square and sturdy. His hands were big; so big as to appear disproportionate with the rest of the body.

Before leaving the room to follow his father, Karmenu unbolted one of the window shutters and peeked out through the glass. It was a damp morning and behind the foggy window, he saw the bay wrapped in a curtain of mist, stretching from his nose to the open sea.
Why was his father taking him with him on such a horrible day?
The answer arrived a moment later.

"Happy Birthday" said Ġorġ from behind him.
He had almost forgotten. That day he was turning eight.
"Thank you!" replied Karmenu.

When Karmenu and his father reached the port, the sun had just started brightening the day. The mist had thinned, but the cold was still clammy and damp. The small boat that his father borrowed from the church waited silently at the side of the port. It was rounded in shape and tapered at one end like the shell of an almond. Its aquamarine colour was peeling off, revealing patches of blue underneath it.

Helping his father to lower the boat into the water, Karmenu felt a sense of pride. It was his first time on the boat without his brother.

By midday, they had moved along the rocky coastline of the island, cast the nets and emptied the two lobster creels that his father had anchored the previous week.
The day was passing more rapidly than Karmenu had expected. Then, at around four o'clock, his father had pointed the little boat in the direction of the open sea. Soon the coast of Gozo had become a thin, straight line, starting and ending in sea and so small that stretching his arm out, Karmenu could cover the sight of the island with just his outstretched fingers.
Then, just as dusk began to fall, his father had brought the boat to a halt.

"Pass me the buoy, Karm!"
Reacting to his old man's order, Karmenu passed his father one of the three empty paraffin tanks that sat at the front of the boat. In return, he received a smile, followed by a nod.

The unlit cigar his father had placed between his lips tottered and his eyes returned to the sea.

Sitting at the front of the boat, Karmenu observed his father in silence. He felt the wind brushing over his back and the wooden plank beneath his backside pressing onto his bones.
He looked at the island, so distant across the water, then eyed the coming darkness, which slowly conquered the whole sky.
He was feeling cold.
On the opposite side of the boat, his father had started tying a rope to the buoy.
Unconcerned by the impending darkness, he worked slowly, with his glasses and eyes both pointed towards his hands. He secured a stone to the end of the rope, and meeting Karmenu's eyes he threw the stone into the sea.
The stone disappeared beneath the water surface.
As the slithering rope reached its end, Karmenu's father held the white tank in his hands then placed it over the water surface with a calm gesture. At first, the white tank floated beside the boat's edge, then, as the waves got hold of it, it slowly moved away in the direction of the setting sun.

What followed would remain one of Karmenu's most vivid memories.

"Jump!" ordered his father calmly.
Karmenu looked confused and smiled. Is this a joke?

"Jump into the water!" repeated his father.
This time Karmenu knew his father meant it. It was not a joke. His father never joked.
But jumping into the water?

Paralysed, he looked at his father's dry mouth hoping to find the faint shadow of a smile.

He didn't find it.

He was not jumping.

"No," he said tentatively, plucking courage from his fear. His voice came out like a squeak, revealing all the fear he felt of his father. He was afraid. He had seen his father's anger before and was aware that his refusal could trigger the man's fury.
It did.

"I said, jump into the water!"
This time his father's voice was hard and as solid as a brick wall.
The initial calm in his father's tone had been replaced by anger; the same anger that Karmenu could see in his father's eyes.

Under the direct glare of his father, Karmenu's face crumpled into a silent cry.
Where was Ġorġ when he needed him?
His brother was the only person who could face his father's anger. Not even his mother managed to face his father the way Ġorġ did.

Karmenu tried to stop crying but more and more tears clotted his eyelids. Everything went blurry.
His trembling hands grabbed his jacket to undress. His lips were pressed in a tight grip.

"Don't undress," ordered his father "jump as you are!" he shouted, spacing each word into an even harsher tone.
What have I done? thought Karmenu.
Hadn't he helped casting the nets and done everything he'd been asked to do? Why was he being punished?

"It's my birthday," he whispered, and more tears breached his eyelids. But his father stood up, he staggered two steps across the boat and towered over him.
"Do you want to jump or do I have to throw you in myself?" he mumbled with his unlit cigar dancing beneath his large framed glasses.
Karmenu whined, then felt the grip of his father's hand tightening around his right shoulder and knew he could no longer escape. He closed his eyes and screamed. The other hand reached under his right knee and a moment later, he was swung into the air.

The moment his body hit the water, Karmenu stopped crying. He heard the splashing sound of his feet shattering the sea's surface then felt the tight grip of the water wrapping around him.
The water was cold and as it penetrated his clothes, it felt like ice, burning and freezing at the same time.
A second passed before he was able to move. The water reached every corner of his body and as it reached his face, Karmenu felt his tears being washed away from his eyes. His head sank under the surface of the water and he decided to swim.
He tried to move his feet first but felt like being dipped in a pool of mud. Filled with water, his shoes had become heavy and for every thrust to reach the surface, he felt an equal force pulling him down to the depths.
As his mouth finally managed to reach the surface, he breathed in as deeply as he could, then coughed. With his eyes still shut, he then fought to remain with his mouth above the surface of the water.
He should have shouted for help, but knew that the only person who could hear him was the last person he wanted help from.
I am going to die, he thought.

As his coughing fit reached an end, he opened his eyes.

The sun was dipping, shining through the drops of water caught in his eyelashes. Turning around, he saw his father pulling on the oars and the boat moving away from him.

For a moment, Karmenu observed the boat slipping away, then shouted.
"Please, don't go away!" He screamed as his father kept rowing, but his lungs froze and the scream died in his mouth.

He was alone.

Gathering all his strength, he swam towards the white tank and embraced it with both hands.

A few minutes later the boat had disappeared and for however much he squeezed his eyes all he could see were droplets of water, the sea and the sky.
Then darkness crept in.

With night came fear and the certainty his father would not return. Imaginary sea creatures filled his thoughts. Creatures observing him from the bottom of the sea, whispering his name and waiting for the right moment to attack him. Creatures with long tails and sharp teeth which ate everything and left no remains.

Karmenu clutched the empty paraffin tank and trembled. He would die at sea, he thought, on his eighth birthday.
He cried, and underneath his trembling body, the creatures of the sea listened to his sobs.

He also prayed to the Virgin Mary, to Jesus and to the Lord, just as he'd learned at the Oratory.
"God save me!" he whispered, "I will be good. Please save me." He pleaded, then his thoughts started getting confused and his teeth started chattering.

When his father lifted him back onto the boat, Karmenu was semiconscious.
Taking his time, he took Karmenu's wet clothes off, then, with care that could have been mistaken for love, he wrapped him in a dry towel and rubbed his skin to warm him.
"You are a man now," he whispered.

Karmenu stared at him.
He felt neither hate nor fear. Emptiness was the only word that could describe the way he felt. He dreamt of being in bed with the blankets pulled over his head and his hands hidden between his knees.

CHAPTER 18

BLOOD.

There is a thin line that separates life from death, but once it's crossed, it becomes as large as an ocean.

By the morning of the fourth day, the hope of finding Ġorġ alive had died. Wherever his body was, its soul was no longer with it.

Unlike his uncle Karmenu, Dwardu had not gone out to sea searching for his father. Since his return to the island, he had remained home.
Lights off, he sat on the floor listening to the silence that permeated the house.
The floor was cold and uncomfortable, but neither the comfort of the sofa nor the straight posture of the wooden chairs suited his state of mind. He felt troubled, tired, haunted, angry and disheartened. His body was hurt, his thoughts distant and his very soul cracked and blank.

Since his return, Karmenu, had asked him more than once to go out to sea in search of his father.
He had declined, telling him that he was still afraid; that his back hurt; that the lightning had shaken him and

that the dark sky and the rippling water still frightened him deeper than he could explain.

But it was neither the fear nor the pain that had kept him away from the sea, but a torpor that had fallen upon him, chaining him to the house.

Besides Karmenu, he had seen only his grandmother. At night he heard her weep and by day she moved through the house like a ghost through light.

The knowck on the door woke him. He had gone to bed fully clothed and had slept through the morning.

"Who is it?" he shouted through the house.
"Mario Agius." said the voice of the police inspector.

It was no courtesy visit, realized Dwardu.

"We need to talk, Dwardu! Please let me in," said *spettur* Agius as Dwardu opened the door.
The inspector was dressed in plain clothes, his belly bulging through a white t-shirt and his hands in the pockets.

They sat at the kitchen table, face to face, on opposite sides of the small wooden table.
"I don't know how to tell you ..." started Agius. He stared at his own hands for a long minute, then took a big breath "why don't you first tell me what happened to your father? This time you have to tell me everything, Dwardu. I need you to be precise. Don't get me wrong. I am wearing plain clothes, but I will have to make a report of anything you tell me."

Everything, thought Dwardu. But everything didn't exist. It was just his memory full of gaps that he himself could not fill.

"I'll try," he said.
He spoke slowly, staring at the kitchen wall. He described the rain that had kept pouring over the *Anna Marija* and the mist that had enfolded them and hid them from the rest of the world.
Agius listened. Once or twice, he asked a short question, but mostly he nodded, silently, without interrupting.

"What happened then?" asked Agius.

"I don't know how long we remained anchored to the buoy. It felt like being numb or unconscious. The boat floated and we floated with her. The boat slept or pranced, so did we.

"Was your father still with you when the lightning struck?"
Dwardu nodded.

"We found a lot of blood in the boat."
"I've cut myself," said Dwardu raising his right hand to touch the back of his head.
"There is more blood than the cut could justify."
Blood?
"You mean ... my father's blood?"
"We don't know yet."
"Am ... I being accused of something?"
"No," replied Agius, "but I have to ask you not to leave the island."

That afternoon, for the first time in three days, Dwardu left the house and realised that everything had changed. Everything. The bay, the port, the boats, the sea, the hills, the people; nothing had remained the same.

He walked across the bay for a long time, measuring each step. He stopped at the port. He sat on the tarmac beside the port's wall, crossed his legs and stared at the boats.

Dwardu had only one vivid memory of his mother and he had always kept it to himself. He had just a few photos of her, less than a dozen black and white pictures with a white, rimmed border and fading tones.
Three of these photos portrayed his mother with her family, when she was still young, before she had met his father. Others had her smiling in the school among her pupils and a few more portrayed on her wedding day.
There was only one photo that portrayed the two of them, mother and son, together, and for obvious reasons Dwardu loved it above all.

Photos are still moments of life; they show a slice of the past but don't stir or breathe or hurt as memories do.

In his one, most treasured memory of his mother, Dwardu was about three years old.

July 1962
It was around midday and he had been playing all morning on the terrace sorting and piling some pebbles he'd collected from the beach.
The day was bright and hot, and his mother had told him to sit in the shade, beneath the white sheet she had purposely pinned horizontally between two of the laundry lines.
It was just the two of them. His father was out, probably at sea, and neither his grandmother nor his uncle Karmenu were around.
As he played, his mother hung the laundry in the sun.

Dwardu was still playing with the stones when his mother had gone downstairs, taking with her the empty washtub with her. Dwardu knew how it worked. His mother would have filled the washtub with more clothes and would have come back a few minutes later. So, for the next minutes, he waited for his mother's return. He arranged the pebbles in a row and occasionally looked at the door that connected the house to the terrace.
It had a small doorway, big enough for him but too small for any adult to pass through without having to stoop.
After waiting for some time, he decided to make his way downstairs.
Moving down the spiral staircase, he remembered calling his mother and receiving no answer.
She had abandoned him, he remembered thinking.

Then, almost like a whisper, his mother's voice had reached him from the opposite side of the house.
Forgetting his urge to pee, Dwardu had walked through the narrow corridor.
His mother was by the entrance door talking to someone that he could not see.
"Mum," he had called her.
His mother had not answered him. Instead her voice had risen to a scream.
"Go away," she had shouted. "Go away! I don't want to see you ever again!" She had screamed at the top of her voice. And immediately after, she had slammed the door with such violence that the whole house had shaken like a jelly.

It had taken years for Dwardu to understand who had been at the door.

CHAPTER 19

SKETCHES.

The 'Blue Bell' restaurant, on the road to the saltpans, was a small restaurant with low ceilings and old sepia coloured photographs hanging on the walls. The owners, Maria Vella and her daughter Josie, kept it open from April to November and closed during the winter months when there were scarcely any tourists visiting that part of the island.
The 'Blue Bell' was never full. When anyone searching for a place to eat ventured as far as the saltpans, they normally went to the restaurant nextdoor with its large terrace and all day pizza menu.

Sarah had worked in the 'Blue Bell' for almost five months. Initially employed as waitress for the summer season, she had ended up performing all kind of tasks, from buying groceries to cleaning pans and dishes, to occasionally cooking some of the specialities of the house.

By the end of summer, Sarah had become such an integral part of the little restaurant that Maria and her daughter had asked her to stay longer, until the winter break, and she had accepted.
Sarah loved the place. She loved the white, plastered walls, uneven and full of old rusted nails. She loved the little kitchen with its old gas cooker and its chequered, red and white curtains draping the windows. But most of

all, she loved the nearby pebbled beach, filled with dry seaweed in winter and with loud families in summer.

It was a Tuesday afternoon and no customers had stopped for lunch. Maria and Josie had passed their time listening to the local radio station playing old classics and tattling about the special relationship that linked nature to God, and Sarah had cleaned the tables and watched the sea.
At two o'clock, with the radio still on, they had decided to start switching everything off. A few minutes later, the welcome board was brought inside and the *Closed* sign was hung on the glass door.

"See you tonight!" said Sarah, closing the restaurant door behind her.
"See you tonight, *ħanini,*" Maria had answered from behind the counter.

As always, Sarah walked home.

Observing the rugged coastline, Sarah pondered on how, in the last year, everything had changed so radically that she could hardly recognise herself.
Gone was her life full of lies and subterfuges, and gone were all those false friends who had turned their back on her when she had most needed them.
Her new life was simple and beautiful; full of long walks, quiet evenings and colourful brushstrokes.
It was not the life she had dreamt of but it made her happy, happier than she had ever been before.

Once home, Sarah had gathered her charcoals and her drawing block and had hurried towards the port.
There was a beautiful light. The morning rain had left the air clean, and the grey surfaces were wet and shiny. The sunrays fought their way out of the pearly clouds, beaming columns of light onto the distant hilltops.

Once at the port, Sarah sat on a bench beside the slipway and opened her drawing block. She closed one eye and observed the little hamlet transform into a huddle of black and silvery lines that fitted into each other like the pieces of a jigsaw puzzle.
When her eyes found the perfect cut, her left hand started drawing.
She drew the outlines of the port, the dark walls and the water. She sketched the boats and the young man who sat cross-legged by the opposite wall.

She had seen him before. He was one of the fishermen she had often bought fish from. The same one who had sold her two tail-less groupers, telling her the tail had been eaten by some bigger fish, and the same one who had explained to her that a swordfish sold without head was most likely a different fish.
From a painter's point of view, he was a stunning subject, lean, almost bony with a posture, upright yet bowed, which brought together strength and grief.

Soon, Sarah forgot about the opalescent sky and shiny, wet surfaces. Starting a new sketch, she focused her attention only on the young fisherman.
She outlined his figure, drew the long shadows that stretched across his face, wove lines for his worn-out jumper and sketched the bristle of his hair.
Then, as she started her third sketch, the fisherman uncrossed his legs, stood up and moved away.

She was just about to gather her stuff when she saw him coming back and moving towards her. She paused a moment, unsure if to cover her sketches, but he was already there, boarding the boat moored just before her.

Once boarded, turning around, he looked at her. Just for a moment his eyes gazed at the sketches than at her.

He was handsome, his brown eyes were fierce like those of a wild animal but his expression was gentle.
Sarah nodded.

He didn't nod back, but started loosening the strings that tightened the tarpaulin.

When his eyes glanced back at her, Sarah was still observing him. His features were so strong that he embodied the essence of life at sea.
She opened her mouth to ask him if she could make a portrait of him, a real portrait, with oil, on canvas. But the moment her lips parted, his eyes went back to the knots, and Sarah's courage faded.

CHAPTER 20

THE SHARKMAN.

The ghosts of death hovered over Ġorġ's dead body like vultures over a carcass. His corpse floated in the water forty miles north of the island of Gozo, pushed by the currents and whisked by the winds.
He floated face up, his clothes torn, his face pale and his features swollen.

Joseph 'Kelb' Theuma was probably the most famous fisherman in Gozo. He was the man who had once caught a four-metre white shark with just a small harpoon and a fisherman's knife. He had hit the beast with one single strike through the right eye, which had penetrated deep into the animal's brain.
Pictures showing the beast next to its capturer had been published in many books over the years.

In the Maltese Islands, Theuma's name had become some kind of a legend. Occasionally journalists still turned up in Marsalforn in search of the great shark hunter and though most of them went away disappointed, others found exactly what they'd been looking for.
In person, Joseph Theuma was nothing like legendary. He was skinny and small. He had a rat-like face with a thick, long nose, brown unintelligent eyes, dark skin and

protruding teeth. His hair, mostly gone from his crown at the age of twenty, was tied up at the back in a limp, black ponytail that ended on a little tattoo picturing a mermaid. His nickname, once '*Kelb il-baħar*', meaning literally dog-fish or shark, had quickly shrank to 'Kelb', dog.
Though some foreign books still painted him as a fascinating Hemingway's character, in Gozo, Kelb was nothing more than an average fisherman with a shifty character and an inclination to dishonesty.

Five days after the lightning had struck the *Anna Marija*, Kelb received the call he had been waiting for for weeks. The telephone rang briefly, then stopped for a while and eventually rang again.
Sitting in his favourite armchair with his hand already placed on the receiver and his eyes fixed to the dial, Kelb picked up the handset in a hurried movement that almost sent the whole telephone to the ground. His hands were sweating, his mouth was dry and his heart pulsed at double its normal speed.
The telephone wheezed the creaking sounds typical of international calls then the voice Kelb had expected spoke one short word. Then the line went dead.
In the past five years, Kelb had learned to recognise the man's voice, not only from its tone, but also from its briefness and its hardness.
The same telephone call arrived at regular intervals; normally at the beginning of each month, but occasionally on other days. The voice was always similar, brief and concise. There was no need for many words and the man behind the voice did not like to squander any.

"*Domani*" tomorrow, had said the Italian voice before the line had gone dead.

The following day, Kelb woke up earlier than usual. He looked out of the window to check that the sea was calm. He then dressed and went out.
When he arrived at the port of Marsalforn it was not yet daybreak.
In the gloomy light of the early morning, he could see the Magro brothers unloading their pickup truck. There was no one else in the port.

Kelb walked past the three brothers keeping his head down. He reached his boat and boarded it.
Kelb's boat was the only fibreglass boat in the whole port; a cross between a fishing boat and a small, leisure speedboat. He had bought it six years earlier, from an old British man who had left the island. It was not a beautiful boat, Kelb had to admit that, but it was faster than any other in the port.

Three hours later Kelb had reached the stretch of sea that he had nicknamed *Baħar is-Safra*; a small section of water, shallower than its surroundings, which lay about thirteen miles north of the island of Gozo.
It was a clear day, too clear for the purpose he had come for. The Maltese islands, as well as the coast of Sicily, were both visible through a thin veil of grey mist. To the East, a bulky green cargo-ship balanced on the horizon, crossing from North to South. It was distant enough, Kelb thought. Farther to the North, a much smaller white boat sailed in the opposite direction.
The rest was sea, clouds and distant lands.

Kelb waited. It was a day of *għarixa*, full of fast moving clouds that glided smoothly across the sky.

It was almost one o'clock when a fast, white speedboat moved into view. There they are, thought Kelb. A few

minutes later, Kelb was able to recognise the two men aboard the vessel.
He knew both of them: Nico and Salvatore; both Italians and both police officers in the Italian forces.
Keeping an eye on the speedboat, Kelb took a deep breath and tried to look more relaxed than he felt.
The approaching vessel reduced its speed and drifted towards Kelb's boat.
Kelb nodded and the two men grinned in return.
They were an unlikely pair. Though they both wore sunglasses and dark, padded jackets, they looked very different from one another. Salvatore, the taller of the two, was as skinny as a rail; he had blondish hair and a nose that would have made a Roman emperor proud. The gun he carried was in plain view, attached to his belt and wrapped in its white sheath.
It was loaded, Kelb knew it, as in more than one occasion Salvatore had aimed the gun straight at him and had eventually shot in the water, possibly just for the fun of seeing his reaction.
Of the two men, Salvatore was the muscles.
The brain was Nico.
Nico was short, roughly as tall as Kelb, but heavier and with a stronger build. His neck was as thick as that of a bull and his hair was short, curly and shiny black.
Nico talked little, and when he did, a little lisp made his voice sound less brutal than expected. He kept his gun partially concealed, beneath his jacket.
Of the two, he was the one Kelb feared more.

"*Joseph, ti fai sempre più brutto*! Joseph, you get uglier each time!" shouted Salvatore, laughing at his own joke.

Once the two boats were secured to one another, Nico gave a quick look around, then lifted one of the speedboat's seats and gestured to his companion to draw out whatever was stored in the concealed compartment.

Salvatore picked the first crate of *lampuki and* sneering, handed them over to Kelb with a fast movement.
Kelb's arms outstretched and his face contorted in a disgusted expression. The fish were at least three days old: the eyes of the *lampuki* had sunk and lost most of their brightness, their tails were stiff, like glued up paintbrushes, and the stench the crate emanated was almost unbearable.
Rotten fish had never been part of the deal but he knew better than to complain about it.

The following three crates were no better.
There was no way he would be able to sell that fish at the market. He would have to dump the whole lot at sea, he thought.
In the past five years, he had grown accustomed to the extra cash he made from selling the fish contained in the crates, yet the *lampuki,* the *vopi,* the swordfish, or whichever fish the two men handed him over, were only the most marginal part of the deal. What lay underneath the fish was the real deal.

"*Ha detto Giulio che questa la devi nascondere bene.* Giulio said to hide it well," said Nico pointing his finger at him "He is gonna call you in a couple of weeks. No cock-ups!"

Like most Maltese people, Kelb understood Italian having learnt it by watching programs on the Italian state television, which was usually better and had a clearer signal than the only Maltese channel.
"*No problema, io conosce posto dove nascondere bene,*" he replied to the two men in his best Italian.
"No problem, I know where to hide it."
Both men nodded.
"*Stamme bene*! Good bye!" said Salvatore. He then collected the rope that had tied the two boats and started winding it between his thumb and the right elbow.

A moment later, Nico switched on the engine and in less than five minutes, the two police officers and their speedboat disappeared from the horizon.

Relieved that the part he most feared was over, Kelb observed the distant coast of Sicily and, with his heart still thumping in his chest, he lit a cigarette and sat on the boat's thwart.

As the cigarette burned, Kelb relaxed.
He had graduated to drug courier, he thought.
It wasn't something he liked or something he had ever planned. It had just happened. The cigarette smuggling had led to the smuggling of relics and eventually to drugs. All he had done was play along. Besides, he couldn't really refuse. Once in, there was no easy way out.
Plus, of course there was the money; and the money was good. One delivery paid as much as a month of hard work and the fish was an extra bonus. When it was fresh.

After glancing all around the horizon, Kelb gazed at the four crates of withered fish that rested between his feet. There were about twenty *lampuki* in each crate; slim in shape and blue in colour with a touch of yellow rimming their flanks. They all faced the same direction; their mouths open, their tails stiff and their eyes blank. He crouched over them, picked the first one from the closest crate and shoved it into the sea.
He didn't look where the fish landed, he just listened to the splash and cursed himself for ever getting involved in such a murky business.
Then, without thinking about it further, he slid his right hand between the remaining blue-coloured fish, moving through the gluey scales and fins, and reaching the thin plastic bag that lay hidden beneath them.

For a few seconds he gently fondled the bag. He could feel a drop of sweat rolling past his shoulder blades.
He moved his wrist in a swirling motion and peaking through the fish's tails, he saw the small plastic package. He took it out. It was transparent and its content looked like nothing more than white, pure flour. On each side of the bag were two sets of large, blue numbers. 2455 and 434.
Identification numbers? To Kelb they meant nothing.

Kelb was about to put the bag back inside the crate beneath the fish, when a dull noise coming from the front of the keel froze his empty smile.
The boat rocked slightly and his heart jolted inside his chest.

With a fast, instinctive movement, Kelb hid the bag back beneath the layer of fish. The first thought that came to his mind was: Police. But a quick glance around him was enough to reassure him that except for the sea there was nothing for many miles around.

Yet something had hit the boat; a piece of wood probably, he tried to reassure himself.
With his mind still in alarm, he stood, as the same dull thud reached him one more time.
Again, the boat wobbled and again Kelb's heart froze.

"A piece of wood," he mumbled to himself. It had to be, he thought.
He inhaled a deep breath into the stale smell of fish and moved one step forward to peek over the boat's railing.
What he saw was a bare, unnaturally white human foot, floating in the water just beneath his boat.
Kelb's eyes widened and his breath died in his lungs.

Unable to move, with his eyes fixed on the white-bluish foot that emerged from the side of the boat, Kelb blinked.

Then, leaning a few more inches towards the water, he saw the rest of the washed-out body attached to the foot.

Before he was able to think straight, his thoughts went to Xerri, the fisherman who had disappeared five years earlier and whose body had never been officially recovered.
In his confused state of mind, the connection between the Italian smugglers and Xerri's death was too evident for him to associate the body with anyone else.
Then, looking at the disfigured face of the corpse, he recognised Ġorġ Muscat.

CHAPTER 21

ANNA MARIJA MEETS RICHARD.

July 1954.

The city of Victoria, the capital of the island of Gozo, was still referred to by its original, semitic name: Rabat.
In older times, when the knights still ruled the islands, the city had mainly been concentrated inside the fortified walls of the old citadel, perched on the highest hill.
Eventually, as the threat of the Turks had slowly lessened, the city had spread down the hill growing into an intricate maze of streets and passageways that unfolded around what would then become the church of St. George.

Anna Marija and her family lived in a small blind alley not far away from the church.

Anna Marija closed the door as silently as she could. The spring bolt slid slowly over the small, metal plate then clicked softly, locking the door and leaving her on the outside of the house, in the narrow alley that locals called il-Mandraġġ.
Cautiously, she pushed the door with the tip of her fingers, to make sure it was shut, then, with her fingertips still touching the door, she remained motionless with her ears alert, listening to each and every sound permeating the small alley.

Through the wooden shutters of the next-door house, she could hear the relentless clinking of her grandmother's knitting needles. More clattering noises, probably of dishes, came from the house of one of her aunts, two doors down.
Coming from behind the small door that led to the barn, she could hear the muffled bleating of the small herd of goats that her grandfather kept in his backyard. Then there was the far-away pealing of the church bells and the distant sound of a band playing a march.
It was not right, she thought, to hear no sound coming from her house.
As on every Saturday, her mother had gone out to visit her family in the village of Sannat and her two sisters had gone with her but her father was still at home.
Waiting a little longer, Anna Marija leaned even closer to the entrance door, then eventually the sound she'd been waiting for reached her eardrums through the door's wooden surface.
It was the low rasping sound of her father's snoring; regular and muffled, yet, to her, unmistakable.
A glimmer of a smile crossed her lips then, as fast as she had sneaked out of the door, she slipped through the dark alleys and vanished in the direction of the church.

Anna Marija knew that it was never good for a lady to arrive early for a date; yet she walked quickly, scurrying through the narrow streets in the direction of St. George's square.
The previous night, confessing her thoughts to her diary, she had written that she was in love for the first time; and that she knew that it was so from the way her heart pounded in her chest with such a strength that she could almost hear its beats echoing throughout the room.
As she reached one of the alleys that poured into the square, she realised there was no way she could pass through the gathering crowd unnoticed. It was a feast day

and people from all over the island were swar
town.

Besides being the focal point of the feast, Pjazza *St. George, with the basilica on one side and shops on the remaining three, was at the time the most important square in town.*
As Anna Marija reached the sidewall of the church, a few yards away from the pjazza, *she stopped for a second then entered one of the small blind alleys that surrounded the basilica.*
Again, she looked around, then drew from her small bag a little white mirror and her newly acquired lipstick, the latest in fashion accessories.
Had her father seen her at that moment he would have probably slapped her face and sent her back to her room for the rest of her life.
Her father disapproved of anything that was modern.
He was stuck in the twenties, and had it been up to him, women would still be wearing the għonnella, *the Maltese equivalent of the burka, the garment worn by women in Arab countries.*
Looking in the small mirror, she applied the lipstick with gentle movements, making sure not to waste it.
"Ah, I wish I looked like Linda Christian" she thought.
Linda Christian, the wife of the actor Tyrone Power, was in Anna Marija's opinion the most beautiful woman in the world. She had charm, looks, money and a beautiful husband.
"Nothing I have," she thought again.
Anna Marija looked one last time in the mirror then walked to the square.

She saw him immediately. Standing motionless on the side of the square opposite the church's entrance. He was the tallest person in the square, and without any doubt the most handsome.

His face was full of freckles, his eyes green and his hair short and nicely combed. His light brown, almost blond hair made him stand out in the midst of so many Maltese people like a dove among crows.
It was impossible not to see him, thought Anna Marija, and again she realised how foolish she had been to decide to meet him in such a public place.

He had not seen her yet. He looked around, lost, in an almost nervous way.
"He is looking for me" thought Anna Marija, and with a sinful sense of pride, she smiled and felt her chest redden beneath her dress.

"You are never, ever going to see that young man again!" Her father had yelled the previous evening.
But there she was.

Anna Marija and Richard had met for the first time in that same square just the previous day.
"Pardon me," the young man had said, "could you tell me the way to the Citadel?"
Anna Marija had looked at the tall English man who had placed himself before her and had visibly reddened. He was handsome, she thought, and immediately felt the eyes of every person in the square looking at her.
"Go through that small street," she had said, hastily pointing at St. Joseph Street, "then cross the square and walk up the hill. It's very easy, you can't miss it."
She then stood for a second too long, looking into the young man's eyes and pointing towards the northern exit of the square.

He was in his early twenties, probably one of the many soldiers stationed in the village of Għasri, by the lighthouse.
"Why don't you come with me? You could be my guide." the young man had replied in an English that sounded too fast and too perfect.
Anna Marija was staggered. Talking to a young foreigner in the middle of the main square was enough to start a scandal, let alone walk with him throughout the old citadel.
"I cannot." she had said hurriedly. Then, before the young man could react, she mumbled a good-bye and started walking towards one of the local grocers.

As she had reached the entrance of the shop, Anna Marija had turned around to face the square. The young Englishman was still there, looking at her. Blushing, Anna Marija had first pretended to be looking elsewhere then had hurried inside the shop.
Looking at the tomatoes, aubergines and figs, Anna Marija could thing of nothing else but the tall Englishman; and decided she would visit the Citadel.
Furtively, Anna Marija had slipped out of the shop. She had moved along one of the small side streets behind the former post office and had walked up to the old fortress.

The Citadel, built at the beginning of the seventeenth century by the Knights of St. John, was the most remarkable architectural site in the whole island. Built right in the centre, it commanded a great view of most of the small island.

Anna Marija found the tall young man leaning over the parapet of St. Michael's Bastion looking down at the town. He was alone, and there was no one else around.
"Do you still need a guide?" Anna Marija had asked, trying to sound more adult than her seventeen years.

The Englishman had turned around surprised, and the glitter Anna Marija had seen in his eyes had repaid her for all the boldness she had needed to follow him.
"My name is Richard" the tall Englishman had said, reaching out with his hand.

An hour later, the two of them had walked through the entire Citadel, had read the old graffiti left on the bastion walls, had listened to the mechanical clatter that preceded the pealing of the church bells and had leaned over every parapet to see the view over each part of the island.
During that hour, Anna Marija learnt many things about the tall Englishman.
He was twenty-two years old. He came from Cornwall in the South West of England and had arrived in Gozo three weeks earlier.
Like her, Richard enjoyed literature and poetry. His favourite authors were Fleming and Oscar Wilde. He disliked reading Shakespeare but enjoyed watching his plays, particularly when they were played by professional actors, who made the plots seem even more complex than they already were.
He played the guitar and sometimes he wrote poetry.

"I'd like to see you again" Richard had said on their way down from the Citadel "when can we meet?"
Then he had tried to take her hand, but Anna Marija had evaded him.
Before answering, Anna Marija had hesitated for a moment then she had surprised herself for a second time.
"Tomorrow night." She had replied with a million thoughts moving around her head. "I will see you at the feast."
"Where? At what time?"
"Wait for me in St. George's square, where you met me earlier, by the grocer. I will see you there at seven o'clock."

On her way home, Anna Marija had stopped again at the grocer and had entered the house pretending nothing had happened. Yet, the news of her afternoon walk around the Citadel had preceded her on her way home; Mr. Debattista, her former history teacher, had seen her walking in the company of a tall, foreign man and had mentioned it to a neighbour who had then told her mother. "Do you know what people will think of you?" her mother had said almost in tears, "You are the talk of the town."

Then her father had come back from his workshop and things had worsened.

St. George's square was full of people in their best clothes. The band had started preparing to play the fanfare and coloured pieces of paper flew like butterflies from the church's belfry.

Watching Richard in the far corner of St. George's Square, Anna Marija felt her legs getting weaker. There were so many people around. How had she been so stupid?
Yet, she had gone so far and she was not going to go back now.
Then suddenly she had an idea; Villa Rundle, she thought, the city gardens.
She crossed the square slowly, moving around its edges and occasionally greeting or talking to acquaintances. As she reached Richard from behind, she brushed next to him, and holding a hand to her mouth, she whispered to him to follow her, keeping at a distance.

Anna Marija led Richard through people and buildings. Then, passing one of the pastizzi *stands in Racecourse Street, a hand had touched her shoulder.*
She knew the hand did not belong to Richard as a few seconds earlier she had clearly seen him ten or more yards behind her.

For a moment, she considered ignoring the touch; but what if it was a relative or a schoolteacher?
She turned with a rapid movement, and as she followed the retreating hand, to her surprise she saw a person she hadn't talked to in ages.
He was a young fisherman from the bay of Marsalforn.
Anna Marija had known him during her primary education, but that was a long time before and now, she could no longer remember his name. They had seen each other at Sunday mass the previous week, she recalled, yet his name was still lost in the depth of her memory.
The fisherman looked at her with his one good eye slightly closed. He smiled. His face was clearly embarrassed, yet his smile was gentle.
Anna Marija said nothing but replied with a similar bashful smile. As the silence protracted, Anna Marija could not help noticing that the fisherman's hair was badly combed, the white shirt he was wearing had a dark spot right on his chest, there was sweat on his forehead and there was a black tuft of hair peeping out of his shirt's collar. Then, she observed his left eye, scarred and vacant, which made it hard to look at him straight in the eyes.
Standing among a hundred people wearing their best Sunday dress, he looked like some kind of scarecrow.

Anna Marija waited for the fisherman to say something. Out of the corner of her right eye, she could see the tall figure of Richard slowly advancing in their direction.
As the silence extended a few more seconds she decided to smile again and turn around to continue her escape. She was about to move away when the fisherman started talking.
"Hi Anna Marija" he said in a soft hissing voice. "There is a party tonight on Ramla beach, I saw you and I thought that maybe you ... would like to come."
Ramla "il-Ħamra" was the largest beach on the island of Gozo; its red sand and its gentle dunes had made of it the

most cherished beach of the island. Many books referred to it as the beach of the nymph Calypso, where Ulysses, the hero of the war of Troy, had been swept ashore and had remained for seven years.
"I don't know," replied Anna Marija, not knowing how to decline the invitation, "I would like to come, but I must check with my friend."
Richard had in the meantime reached them by the pastizzi *stand and was now standing right beside them.*

CHAPTER 22

KELB.

Kelb had left the body of Ġorġ Muscat where he had found it; in the open sea, drifting with the currents.
After watching it with a terrified expression on his face, he had pushed it away from the boat with an oar, then had started the engine and had escaped as fast as he could manage.
Moving away, he had turned around twice, once to make sure the body had remained where he had last seen it, and the second time to murmur a few silent words and make the sign of the cross.

For most of the journey back to the island, Ġorġ's decomposing body had remained stuck in his thoughts. By the time he managed to get rid of such a horrid vision, Kelb had completely forgotten about the wooden crates of rotten fish hiding the drugs.
He remembered them when he had almost reached the coast of Gozo. With the island stretching vastly over the horizon, he had stopped the boat and dumped the foul-smelling fish.

At night the vision had returned. As soon as he closed his eyes, the mangled, white face of Ġorġ's lifeless body appeared before him keeping him awake.
By morning, his fingers twitched and his eyes squinted at every gleam of light. Soon after, he was out of the house.

He had to tell somebody, he thought, and had started walking towards the church.

Once he reached it, he stopped. He hadn't set foot in a church for over twenty years.

September 1958

The village of Xagħra, on the eastern flank of Marsalforn had three churches, two smaller chapels and a vast number of niches and statues dedicated to saints. During the village feast on the weekend proceeding the 8th of September, all of them were lit and decorated as tradition dictated.

At the age of seventeen, Kelb was not yet a shark hunter. He wasn't even a fisherman. People still called him Joseph; and when they wanted to be scpecific, they identified him as Joseph the son of Rina.
He lived with his mother and his twin sister in a one-storey house, owned by the church where his mother worked as housekeeper.
Joseph too helped in the church. He was an altar boy; he helped preparing for the festive events and carried the wooden cross during the Good Friday procession.
When he didn't help out in the church, he worked as a scavenger for the government.

In town, everyone knew him. His work as a street cleaner was to run around the village collecting the garbage left outside each household and nobody did it faster than him.
Like most kids of his generation, Joseph went around barefoot; his only pair of shoes kept for Sunday mass and other events. Yet, shoes or no shoes, at the age of seventeen, Joseph could run faster than anyone else in the

village. His skinny, short body seemed to have been designed for fast speed.
Otherwise, Joseph was a very normal youth; an average student and a devout Christian.

But things were about to change.

It was the last day of the feast and father Paul was running late for the celebrations.

Patri Pawlu or Father Paul, as his mother always called him, was a fat man with plump rosy cheeks, bulging eyes and receding white hair; his forehead was large and pink and Kelb could recall him endlessly wiping it with a white handkerchief. At times, he wore glasses with an enormous frame that rested on his face like goggles, making his eyes swim left to right like goldfish in a beer glass.
He was a good priest and young Joseph adored him.
Despite his dumpy appearance, Father Paul was a lively person, with many interests and a good sense of humour.
To Joseph he was the father figure he had missed since his early childhood. He had been only five years old when his father had emigrated to Australia and eight years old when he had died.

The village had been decked out with festoons, flags and statues of saints. Members of the band gathered around the main square to rehearse their fanfare and the first pedlars had set up their stalls full of candies, dried figs and dates.
It was mid-morning when Joseph entered Father Paul's house. In those times, it was rare for anyone to lock the house doors, so Joseph entered the priest's home without knocking. After all, if Father Paul was late, it was possibly his fault. He had lost track of time looking in the mirror at his Sunday clothes and had completely forgotten that he had agreed to help Father Paul dress for the feast.

As he had done many times before, Joseph ran up the stairs of the house and after a quick knock on the door, had entered the priest's bedroom.
The room was large, its walls painted white and its furniture dark and heavy. Father Paul's bed was an old 19th century double bed, which had once belonged to the priest's parents and still bore the marks of the bomb that had hit the neighbouring house.
Patri Pawlu lay in bed, naked from the waist down, his face looking at him in total despair.
Lying next to the old priest was Joseph's sister.
She too was shocked; her young breast bulging beneath the priest's right hand and her hair spread all over the white pillow.

His surprise had turned to rage; a rage that Joseph could not manage to contain.

They say that some moments are key to a whole existence. That was Kelb's life-defining moment.

Blind with anger he approached the bed and started hitting the person who, until a moment before, had been his closest thing to a father. He hit him with his bare hands, then with a shoe, then again with his hands. He hit him with all the strength he had in his body. He didn't listen to the screams that came from the man, nor to the shrieks that reached him from his sister. He struck at the priest's half naked body blindly, with all the force he had in himself.
Then he ran away.

That day, Patri Pawlu did not attend the procession.
Rumours went around that he had fallen down the stairs of his house and had broken several of his bones. He wasn't back at the church for many months and was eventually transferred to another parish on the other side of the island.

Only a few priests got to know what had really happened, and they all agreed that Kelb's sister was to be sent to a convent. Kelb's mother had little option but to agree.

As Kelb entered the little church of St. Paul in Marsalforn, many contrasting memories came back to his mind. His eyes lingered on the church's vaults and onto the white plaster of the walls then settled on the figure of Christ.
He never understood how the tormented figure of a man on a cross could bring peace into the soul of a person.

It was six o'clock in the morning, the church bells were chiming and two elderly women, in black clothes and black veils sat on the wooden pews reciting the rosary in a whispering silence. One of them, Kelb realised, was Ġorġ Muscat's mother.
Sitting on a pew closer to the altar, was a young priest, one that Kelb had never seen before.

Making the sign of the cross, Kelb knelt in direction of the altar then walked towards the only confessionary in the church.
The priest arrived a moment later. He entered the small, wooden cubicle, closed the velvet curtain and opened the slit.

"Tell me," came the voice.
"Father I have sinned," said Kelb, remembering the standard formula that started every confession.
"When was the last time you confessed?" asked the priest.
"*Ilu ħafna*, it has been a long time."
"What brought you here today?" asked the clergyman.

Kelb looked at the priest's shadow hidden by the grated window, then plucked up his courage and started talking.
"Ġorġ Muscat," he whispered, making sure nobody else in the little church could hear his words.
"The missing fisherman?" replied the priest unprepared.
"Yes."

Kelb explained how he had seen the body of Ġorġ Muscat floating in the sea somewhere north of the island.
Soon he was talking fast, spurting each word like a deadly sin. For a moment, he wished he could say it all; reveal to the young priest about the cigarette smuggling, and about the relics, and about the drug-trafficking. He wished he could confess to him everything about the Italian policemen, about the husky voice on the telephone and about the threats he received to assure his silence. He almost did. He went as far as to give the exact location of where he'd seen the corpse, but when he was about to confess the reason that had brought him to that far away stretch of sea, he suddenly stopped. He could not trust a priest.

According to the church, a confession is a secret between man and God where the priest is just an intermediary who has neither ears nor eyes. Yet Kelb had learned long before that a priest was first and foremost a man; a person with all qualities and flaws a man can have. That's why he didn't trust priests any more than he trusted his mother. At stake was his freedom. Drug trafficking could cost him a minimum of 10 years in prison, and although his life was dull and grey, he was not ready to sacrifice it to the church.
All he told the priest was about the corpse.

"... his body was so pale and his flesh so swollen that it looked as if his skin would flay apart from the body ...", he said with his eyes closed.

There was some shuffling inside the booth and Kelb realised the young priest was getting uncomfortable. He was, after all, mostly used to old women confessing arguments with their husbands and to teenagers disclosing their first sexual experiences.
“There is no sin in what you are telling me”, said the priest in a serious tone “you should talk to the police, not to God.”
Kelb looked at the dark spots on the red carpet skirting the altar. He had no intention of talking to the police. He had just wanted someone to listen to him. That was all. So, he stood up and walked out of the church.

CHAPTER 23

SIX DAYS ON.

The loss of a loved one is like the loss of a part of oneself; an arm or a leg. At first, the pain is so physical that it is hard to ignore. The trauma is so intense that the mind finds it hard to cope with the loss. With time the pain eases, the body recovers and the brain figures out new ways to go on.

Six days after the lightning, Dwardu's and Karmenu's wounds were still burning.

"What did Agius tell you?" asked Karmenu as he lowered the net into the water.
"Not much!" replied Dwardu from the centre of the boat. "Agius said that the police need to keep the *Anna Marija* for a few more days ... nothing more," he said, and continued rowing.

The two of them had gone out to sea in the early hours of the day, when it was still dark.
At four o'clock in the morning, Karmenu had got out of bed, unable to sleep. Outside it was still dark, but the sea was calm and tempting.
He would have gone out alone, but seeing lights on at his brother's house, he had decided to check on Dwardu.

He had found him awake and fully dressed. His face was sombre and withered like the face of someone who hadn't slept for many days. His beard had grown making him look more like his father.
"I am going out to sea," he had said standing before him at the door "Do you want to come too?"

On the way to the boat, they had passed by the shed and taken nets, lines and creels.

The morning had passed slowly, with each of them absorbed in his own thoughts. Casting the first creels, they had talked little. Then, they had remained silent.

"They say that you killed him," said Karmenu suddenly. His words came out sharp and bitter and unbroken by the wind; they spread around like silence, then waited.
"*Minn qallek?* Who said that?" Dwardu asked.
"Some of the fishermen at the port."

It was inevitable. A small island like Gozo thrived on rumours and it was only a matter of time before someone was bound to accuse him of killing his father.
"And you believe them?" asked Dwardu not hiding his anger.
"I don't know. They might be right. I wasn't there!" replied Karmenu shrugging his shoulders.
"So, you think I killed him?"

Karmenu's hands released a few more metres of net, then closed around one of the orange floats and clasped it hard. He then turned to face his nephew who had stopped rowing and was waiting for his answer. He looks so much like Ġorġ, he thought.

"I don't believe it," he said.

When the old man sat next to her by the port and started speaking in Maltese, Sarah smiled as she always did on such occasions.
With her dark hair and olive skin, Sarah didn't look like a typical foreigner and many people believed she was local.
She had been hoping to see the young fisherman she had sketched the previous day, but he wasn't there.

"*Ġurnata veru sabiħa llum,*" said the old man.
"Sorry but I don't understand Maltese," Sarah interrupted him.
Looking at her with bewildered eyes, the old man stopped talking and let out a loud, cackling laugh followed by coughing fit.
"Sorry," he excused himself, "I didn't realise you were not Maltese." Then he laughed again, and again his croaking laugh ended in a coughing fit.
He was very old, thought Sarah, yet his eyes and his voice were younger than his looks. His English had a trace of Australian inflection, which Sarah had learnt, was a common thing as many Maltese had migrated after the war.
"Where are you from?" asked the man.
"England." replied Sarah.
"You don't look English. You look Maltese."
Sarah smiled. He could not have been more off the mark. Her mother was from Cornwall and her father was Irish, but after almost two years living in Gozo she was getting used to people mistaking her for a local.
"My mother's family was originally from Greece," she said, trying to explain her Mediterranean looks, "but I was born in England."
"Greece!" murmured the old man. "I was there once. There are many Maltese there! They went there to build the windmills. The Maltese windmills were the best in

the world." he said. Then his eyes looked down and he stopped talking for a minute.
"Are you waiting for him?" the old man suddenly asked pointing his finger to the sketch Sarah held in her hands.
It was the portrait of the young fisherman she had drawn the previous day. In the evening, she had added a touch of colour, then, unsatisfied, she had decided to sketch it again, this time with the intention of eventually using it as a study for an oil painting.
She still intended asking the fisherman to pose for her, but was not sure he would accept.
"No, this is just a sketch." said Sarah, reddening, "I don't know him" she continued, her voice trembling.
The old man did not seem to notice her embarrassment; he looked at the entrance of the port and stood up from the bench.
"I think he will be back soon," he said, "he went out this morning, very early, when it was still dark. I think it's his first time out to sea after the tragedy."
Then, as if he had suddenly noticed something he hadn't perceived earlier, the old man looked at Sarah with enquiring eyes.
"You know what happened to Ġorġ Muscat, don't you?"

It was the name of the fisherman who had been lost at sea. She remembered that Maria and Josie had told her that two Gozitan fishermen had been caught in a storm and that only one had come back.
It had never passed through her mind that the man lost at sea could be a person she had seen around. She had grown up in a big country where anything that the news reported normally referred to facts that happened hundred of miles away from where she was.

"If you ask me, it was a damned stupid thing to go out to sea that day," continued the old man.

They remained quiet for some time.

"Do you know his name?" asked Sarah.
"Who's name", replied the old man.
"The name of the fisherman in the portrait," said Sarah reddening a little.
"Oh, him. His name is Dwardu Muscat."

"By the way, I am Sarah," she said extending her hand "what's your name?"
"My name?" asked the man. "My name is Saver, but everyone calls me *Fanal,* like the lighthouse," he laughed.

When Dwardu and Karmenu Muscat returned to the port, it was early afternoon.
Sarah was still sitting on the bench by the side of the slipway and Fanal had gone back to his son's restaurant. Before going, he had invited Sarah to visit him. "I am always there", he had said pointing at the small restaurant at the entrance of the port, "come over any time". Sarah had smiled. "Only if you pose for a portrait", she had replied with the smile still adorning her face. Fanal had looked at her for a second, then he had laughed with his unmistakable loud roar and as he walked away his usual coughing fit started.

Left alone, Sarah had sketched the port once again. It had become one of her favourite subjects. It had it all: beauty, tradition, life. And though the light was not as beautiful as it had been the previous day, the water still glittered and the boats shone in sun.

As the *Ħamra* entered the port, Sarah was no longer drawing. She was looking at the many buildings that skirted the coast on the opposite side of the bay. One of them was where she lived.

The two fishermen secured the boat, then started unloading the crates of fish.

Soon, people were coming out from the restaurants and gathering around the crates. Some of them looked closely at the fish and others waited to see what was left to be unloaded. Words were whispered in ears followed by nods and more whispers.
Then some crates were taken away and others moved to the side.

Eventually only one crate was left, the people dispersed, and the two fishermen moved back onto the boat to collect the lines and the nets.

“Was it a good day?” Sarah asked the two fishermen.
The older of the two men looked at her for a moment, then in an almost shy manner went back to collecting the lines.
Sarah noticed that he had a large scar which extended from his left temple and moved down to his eye. His left eye was discoloured and blind.
It was the younger fisherman who eventually answered.
“It was okay,” he replied, giving her a quick glance and then turning his head back to the remaining crate of fish.
There was nothing charming in the way he replied, but Sarah noticed his eyes pausing over hers for a little longer than she expected.
“Do you normally catch more than today?” Sarah asked again.
This time the answer came back immediately.
“Sometimes,” said the young fisherman lifting the crate and starting moving towards the only van parked in the area.

What a wonderful portrait he would have made, standing against the light with tense arms, holding the wooden crate full of gleaming fish.
Then he stopped. It was his turn to ask questions.
"You live here?" he asked.
Sarah nodded.
"I live on the other side of the bay," she said, pointing to one of the many buildings that looked over the coast.
"You're a painter?"
She smiled. She found it fascinating how direct local people could be.
"It's just a hobby," she replied, thinking this was right moment to ask him to pose for him.
Unluckily, his acknowledgement was just a grunt, a second later, before Sarah could speak, he lifted the crate and walked away across the port.

Sarah observed him moving away, then turned to look at the older fisherman who was decking the boat.
"Is he always so friendly?" she asked with a smile.
The fisherman turned his head towards her but kept tying the green canvas to the boat's ridge.
"Who, Dwardu?" he said in a friendly, calm tone, he then shrugged his shoulders and added, "with him you never know."

CHAPTER 24

RAMLA BEACH PARTY.

July 1954.

Anna Marija had never seen Ramla beach at night.
With the darkness, the orange colour of the sand turned dark grey and the hills around the valley became large and furtive shadows that melted into the sky.
It was a beautiful night. The large bonfire, set in the middle of the beach, burned slowly, shining light over the people and creating moving shadows that looked like an oil painting escaping from its canvas. Not too far away, the statue of the Virgin glowed in the moonlight.
Taking off her shoes, she discovered the refreshing feeling of the chilled sand soothing her feet. Together with Richard she wandered around the dunes spying on night flowers and discovering small paths through the shrubs.
Then something new was added to the evening: music.
"Shall we dance?" asked Richard

They moved to the tunes of Nat King Cole and Frankie Laine, with their bare feet circling on the sand.
Then it happened. Richard kissed her.
Once, then a second and a third time. And on the third time, Anna Marija returned the kiss.
Richard pressed his body against hers and held her so tightly that Anna Marija felt every inch of his body.
He wanted her, Anna Marija could feel it. The pressure of his pelvis against her hips left her with no doubts.

He kissed her more and for longer until he drove her hand from his hip to the front of his trousers. She attempted a timid resistance but his firm hand won the battle easily. She rested her hand on his swollen crotch and feeling a warmth coming from within her, she kissed him more passionately than she had ever kissed before.

A sudden voice from somewhere nearby put an end to their intimacy and they moved away holding hands and walked towards the sea.
They dipped their feet in the water, then sat on the sand by the fire.

They had been sitting for some time, holding hands and talking about their daily lives, when Richard's eyes caught a movement in the distance. He excused himself and was gone.

Twenty minutes later he was not yet back, so Anna Marija decided to look for him.
"Did you see a tall young man? Very tall, with fair hair?" Eventually she was told he had gone away, "He left; ten, fifteen minutes ago, on a motorbike."

He was gone ...without saying a word.

Everything seemed to crumble.

Sitting on the cold sand Anna Marija fought the pressing tears. She had always been too emotional and now she felt like a little girl who'd broken her new present.

The night turned colder.

After some time, someone sat beside her. It wasn't Richard but Karmenu. With a gentle tone he asked her if she wanted to talk.

"I can be your confidant, if you want," he said, and when he received no reply, he asked her if she wanted to go home.
"I know a person with a car," he said, "I can ask him to give you a lift, if you want."
"No thanks," replied Anna Marija, though she really felt like going home.

"Do you mind if I remain here? I will be silent." he asked.

Anna Marija imagined him like a loyal dog, sitting by his master.

Karmenu had remained a little longer then left and returned with a blanket.
"Maybe you are cold," he said.
He then left the blanket next to her and was gone again.

Once Karmenu was far away, Anna Marija put the blanket over her shoulders. It was soft and smelled good, and she wondered who it belonged to.
Suddenly she realised she longed for Karmenu's comforting presence almost as much as she missed Richard. She felt sorry for him; for his scar, for his simple ways and for the way she had treated him.

She looked at the sea and counted the frequency of the white crests closing onto the beach. It had a calming effect. As a young girl, she had once been told that each wave carried a dream from across the sea.

It was then that the evening took a second, unexpected twist.

It had become very late. Anna Marija didn't know exactly how late but knew she was up for a monumental punishment.

Nothing she didn't deserve, she thought; but not for sneaking out of home as much as for having fallen in love with a man whom she didn't know: a solider.

"Hi Anna Marija", said a deep voice she did not recognise. Standing before her was a young man with a dark beard and short hair. It was Karmenu's older brother.

"Can I sit next to you?" he asked with the same soft voice of his brother.
Anna Marija nodded and he sat right beside her.

He remained like that a second, than lay down with his back on the sand.

It was Anna Marija who broke the silence.
"You are Karmenu's brother, right?" she asked.
Before answering, the bearded man shifted his position and sat crossed-legs facing her.

"Yes, my name is Ġorġ," he said extending his hand.
"I am Anna Marija," she replied, shaking his hand.
"I know," he said.

She'd been wrong. His voice was very different from his brother's.
"What happened to the tall Englishman who was with you?" he asked immediately after.
"He's gone!"

She would have added more had her eyes not threatened to let out a river.
"Would you like to go for a swim?" he asked.

Swimming, she thought, at night? And looking at the water she found it too black and frightening.
"But it's night!" she argued.
He smiled.

She had never swum at night and just the thought made her shiver.

"What's wrong with swimming at night?"
That it's dark, she thought.
"The water is too cold!" she said tentatively.
"It's not," replied Ġorġ with a gentle tone and the trace of a smile hidden behind his beard.

He did not insist any further. Without saying another word he stood up, took off his shirt and trousers and ran towards the sea with nothing else but his briefs.
Anna Marija was speechless, first her hand over Richard's body, now this.
No man had ever taken off his clothing in front of her before that day. And though she knew she was supposed look away she didn't, her eyes remained hooked on Ġorġ's back and shoulders until he dived into the water. She found him sexy.

Ġorġ had just earned a place in her diary along Richard, she thought smiling. But her smile froze.
"There you are!" shouted an unmistakable voice.
Oh God! She could have recognised that voice in the middle of a thousand shouting people. It was her father.
How had he found her? How long had he been looking for her?

She was in deep trouble.

CHAPTER 25

SINS.

The first historical records mentioning the little church of Marsalforn dated as far back as the thirteenth century. A Venetian traveler passing through the Maltese islands had described it as a little chapel by the sea dedicated to the shipwreck of the disciple Paul.
The original chapel was long gone, replaced by a more modern version, larger and taller, but still simple in its appearance. Inside, the church had just a few decorations; an old altarpiece representing Saint Paul with a snake attached to his hand and two or three more paintings placed along the nave.

Dun Mikiel *il-Malti*, the parish priest of Marsalforn's little church, lived in a building adjacent to the church. He had moved there five years earlier when he had returned from abroad to be assigned the control of the little parish.
He was a devoted man, good-natured yet austere. He represented the strictest part of religion, one that believed in hardship, discipline and punishment. His sermons often spoke of the rewards of a life dedicated to God and of the many obstacles that one had to overcome.
Dun Mikiel's day followed a strict routine that he rarely ever modified. Part of this routine was his early morning walk. He called it "the hour of air" and since he lived in Marsalforn, it consisted of a long walk along the coast.

As he came out of his house that morning, he was surprised to find Father Pierre waiting for him on the little pavement opposite his house.
Father Pierre was a young priest that the bishop had assigned to help him run the church. He was a pale, delicate man and Dun Mikiel had never liked him too much. To be a priest, one needed not just faith but also discipline, dignity and a strong moral sense. In his opinion, Father Pierre lacked most of these qualities.

"Good Morning, Father!" said Father Pierre as soon as Dun Mikiel came out of the house. "There is one thing that has been troubling me all night."
"Walk with me!" said the older man walking in the direction of the bay.
"So, what is it?" he asked. His tone was dry and his step brisk, almost military. He didn't like to be disturbed during his morning walk.

"A parishioner has informed me during confession that he has seen the body of Ġorġ Muscat." said the young priest.
"The fisherman?"
"Yes, father. I prayed for his soul the whole night. But I didn't know what else to do. That's why I am here."
"When did it happen?"
"What, Father?"
"When did you receive the confession?"
"Yesterday, in the early morning."
"And you are telling me now!" said Dun Mikiel raising his voice just enough to show a distant trace of anger "Why didn't you inform me right away?"
"But Father, yesterday you were in Malta all day."
"You should have told me in the evening, as soon as I returned."
"But, I thought ..."
The parish priest cut him short.
"Who was it? Who told you?"

"But Father, it was a confession!"
"Don't give me that kind of rubbish of 'you say the sin but not the sinner' I am your superior," said Dun Mikiel in a firm tone. "So, if you don't want to end up preaching in some mission in Brazil, you'd better tell me who the person is, now."
"But he made me promise that I wouldn't tell anyone." said Father Pierre in a quivering tone.
"Stop this nonsense. Just tell me his name."
The young priest trembled.
"Kelb."
"Are you teasing me?"
"It's his nickname, Father. His name is Joseph Theuma, he is a fisherm ..."
"I know who he is. He is the smuggler. Isn't he?"
"So I heard."
"So, where is the body?"
"He said, halfway between Gozo and Sicily."
"And what else did he confess?"
"Nothing Father, that was all."
"Ok. Go now. I'll talk to you later."

Returning home Dun Mikiel passed by the police station.

The Marsalforn police station was hardly bigger than a closet; a one-room office furnished with an old wooden desk, a filing cabinet and a window. It was situated just outside the small port, in a vantage point that allowed a view of most of the bay.

"Good morning, Father."
"Good morning. I need to speak to inspector Agius."
"I am afraid he is not here right now ..."

"Then call him and tell him that I need to speak to him urgently. He can find me at home."

When Inspector Agius knocked on Dun Mikiel's door, it was already afternoon.
He was dressed in plain clothes and was in none of the hurry Dun Mikiel had expected to see him in.

"I was expecting you earlier," shouted the priest from the balcony.
"It was very busy this morning. I came as soon as I could," replied the inspector.
"I see," said the cleric and then made a sign to follow him upstairs.

The house of Dun Mikiel was simple. The furniture was old and its walls were bare, except for a metal cross, nailed by the entrance door.

"Yesterday, one of our parishioners confessed to Father Pierre that he saw the body of the missing fisherman out at sea. It must have been somewhere between Gozo and Sicily."
"Oh, you are late, Father. The body may have already been found. The headquarters in Malta received a phone call from Italy this morning. A body fitting Ġorġ Muscat's description has been washed ashore on the Sicilian coast, near the town of Sciacca."
"So, I guess I made you come here for nothing."
"Maybe, not," he paused, "maybe you could tell me the name of the man who saw the body? You know, I might want to ask him some questions."
The priest smiled.
"I knew you would ask," he said, "his name is Kelb."

PART III – Earth

CHAPTER 26

IS-SINJUR.

June 1972.

Dwardu Muscat was just fourteen years old when the people of the island noticed him for the first time.
It was the end of June and school had just ended.

Dwardu was a thin boy whose years without a mother had shaped him into a difficult and troubled teenager. He rarely spoke to anyone, and like his father, he preferred a long day out at sea than a day among his peers.
Although attending school, he had already been working on his father's boat for the last three years, and although he was by no means an accomplished fisherman, he knew more about the sea than he knew about people.

In his spare time, Dwardu built creel fishing-traps called nassi, *which he sold in Rabat on market days.*
Nobody knew what he did with the money he earned from the nassi. *His father never asked and Dwardu never felt the need to say anything about it.*
On rare occasions he bought fresh flowers for his mother's tombstone. Not the tombstone at the cemetery, but a very personal plaque that he himself had carved and placed in a spot up on the hill, hidden from everyone else's eyes. It stated, his mother's name, "Anna Marija", and nothing more.

Yet these gifts claimed only a small amount of the money he earnt, as most of the flowers were taken from nearby fields.

It was on a market day that the trouble began.
The year was 1972. That year, tourists had started discovering the island, Kelb had already caught the shark which would earn him his nickname and Ġorġ and Karmenu were still fishing with one boat.

The smaller arm of the old clock on the bastion had already reached the eleventh hour, and the streets of Rabat were bustling with people from every corner of the island.
Barefoot, lightly clothed and with a battered straw hat carelessly placed on his head, Dwardu sat by the white, worn-out steps leading to the citadel.
Before him, trapped between his legs, was a large creel he had been working on since the previous weekend. On his right were two more nassi; *both completed, yet smaller than the one he was building right then. On his left was a fishing net, which a fisherman from the port had asked him to sell.*

Sitting in the sun, Dwardu worked the reed, gashing and stripping the rods with the precision of a carpenter and binding them with the patience of a tailor.

He had not sold anything that day.
Two people had enquired about the price of the net but no one else had gone further than looking at his work.

As midday approached, Dwardu wiped his nose and forehead with his free hand then continued to fasten the small strips of wood to oneanother.
The sun was starting to bake his arms and legs and rivulets of sweat were trickling down his face. In addition

to that, a herd of goats had left the air full of the pungent smell of mud, sour milk and dung.

"How much for this one?" asked a man in a freshly ironed shirt and leather shoes, pointing at one of the smaller creel.
He was a sinjur, *a rich man from the city; one who could afford to own a nice house, a new car and even an apartment on the main island.*
Dwardu had seen him before, somewhere in Marsalforn, wearing spotless clothes and driving a roofless car but only later he discovered he was Anthony Zammit Caruana, the best known barrister on the island.
"Tmienja, eight" he said, wondering what a fashion-plate like the man before him might do with a fishing device.
Less than a month earlier, the Maltese currency had changed from the imperial unit to the decimal one and most people were still not sure which currency to deal with.
"Are you talking in Liri *or Pounds?" was the fast reply of the man.*
"Pounds." he replied flat-toned.
"Eight Pounds?" the sinjur repeated, looking around as to underline the crazy price the young fisherman had requested." That's too much! How much is the other one, then?" he continued.
Dwardu stopped working. From underneath his hat he glanced at the sinjur, *looking for any trace of mockery perking up his face.*
"L-istess, *it's the same price," replied Dwardu, giving the man an annoyed stare, "they are the same size, can't you see it?"*
The man did not flinch.
"How much is the net, then?"

What the hell did he want now?

"150 pounds." That would have been twenty for himself and the rest for the fisherman he was selling the net for.
"Hundred and fifty?" roared the man, pronouncing each word followed by a little pause "Not even your mother would buy it for that price," he continued, with a thin smile.
It had been a mistake to utter those words and even the sinjur realised it as soon as his lips closed. He tried to move on, but Dwardu had already sprung up from his position. He had pushed aside the nassi *he was working on and had caught the man by his shirt, right over his chest. A second later, too fast for anyone to see, he struck him above the hip.*

Had the sinjur not been wearing a white shirt, the attack would probably not have been so evident but as the white satin fabric started blotting with blood, shouts arrived almost instantaneously.
A moment later, the sinjur was lying on the ground.

Beside him was a young girl, about Dwardu's age. She had black hair and dark eyes. As she leaned to the side of the man, she had looked at Dwardu, who was still holding the blooded knife in his hands. In her eyes was a mixture of fear and condemnation.
Dwardu wished he had seen her before. But it was too late. So, he sat back in his place, he threw the knife on the ground next to the string and resumed work on his large nassi.

When Constable Mario Agius came to arrest him, Dwardu offered no resistance.
He did not deny what had happened. "The man deserved it!" he said quietly, and added no other word until his father showed up at the police station.

That evening, for the first time in his life, his father hit him with his belt and Dwardu accepted his punishment in silence.

One week later he was sentenced to three months in prison.

CHAPTER 27

WOUNDS.

Eight years had passed since the stabbing. Dwardu had grown into a man but people had not forgotten. So, whilst his father was remembered as the fisherman who had lost his young wife, Dwardu was still known as the one who had stabbed *is-Sur Avukat* during the Sunday market.

Now he was about to be arrested again.

In the morning inspector Agius had visited him.
"We have to talk again" he said. "It's not getting any better Dwardu. Let's go in, if you don't mind."

They had moved into the house and sat at the kitchen table.

"There are more problems, Dwardu," Agius said, with his eyes fixed on the table, "the examinations on your father's body have revealed two deep wounds, one above his right temple and another one on his chest." Agius paused for a second then continued, "I have been asked to detain you."
"Am I being accused of murder?"
Agius looked at him and sighed.
"Not yet, but you will have to be questioned."
"But I have already told you everything I know." said Dwardu, standing up. He looked about to explode.
"We need to ask you more questions."

Agius let the silence pervade the room, then went on explaining what the medical examiner had said.
"The wound above his right temple could be the result of an impact of your father's head with something hard, possibly a pointed object. There could be several objects that could have caused that wound," he said, "the real problem is the other wound."
"The medical examiner maintains that it is a knife wound," he continued, "the body is badly decomposed and there is no complete certainty about it. But the wound is deep, and your father's lungs contain traces of blood."

"He might have fallen onto something," said Dwardu with his eyes fixed on the wall.
"Yes, Dwardu, he might have," said Agius, "but where? Did you see him hitting something?"
"I cannot remember, I told you."
"That's the problem. I need you to remember."
"What do you suggest? Do you want me to make up a story, so that I can answer your questions? Is that what the police want me to do?"
"Calm down. Nobody wants you to invent anything, but the fact that you remember nothing of your father's last moments on the boat helps neither the police or yourself."

"So you are arresting me?"
Agius didn't answer immediately, he stood up and paced towards the window.
"Go to your father's funeral first."
Dwardu seemed almost surprised.
"What if I run away?"
Agius studied Dwardu's face, deciding how much trust he was worthy of.
"And go where?"
Agius moved towards Dwardu and shook his hand.

“I will see you tonight then,” he said, “don't disappoint me.”

He then walked towards the door and opened it but stopped before going out.
“One last thing, Dwardu,” said the inspector tending his hand palm up, “I need your knife!”

Dwardu fished in his right pocket, produced a small clasp knife and unwillingly placed it in Agius' hand.

CHAPTER 28

THE FUNERAL.

There is a period for hope and one for mourning.

The funeral ceremony started at four o'clock in the afternoon and lasted for one hour.
At the end of it, four men dressed fully in black marched out of the little church of St. Paul the Shipwreck. On their shoulders was the wooden coffin containing the body of the late fisherman Ġorġ Muscat.

None of the four men would have easily passed unnoticed. One of them was partially blind and had wet eyes from fresh tears. Another one was young and thin, and had a black beard that made him look very much like the deceased. The third one was a young priest, pale and fragile, just strong enough to bear his part of the weight but weak enough to be weeping as he walked through the crowd. The last of the four was a tall man, taller than most of the people around him; so tall in fact that he had to walk uncomfortably, keeping his knees bent and his back bowed, not to unbalance the march of the other three.

Fanal knew all of them. Had he been younger, he too would have been carrying his part of the weight. A weight that as his experience had taught him felt directly proportional to the sins committed in life by the departed. The heavier the coffin the more sins the deceased had committed in life.

Many people followed the four men out of the little church. Soon, the flight of stairs before the church were fraught with mourners squeezing through the door and broadening like a river of black ink spreading on a paper.

There were more people than anyone had expected. Possibly because it was Saturday or maybe because after the many days of fruitless search, destiny had bestowed Ġorġ Muscat with an air of martyrdom. Yet of all the people that streamed behind the coffin, only a handful had really known him.
Most of them identified him only as the silent fishermen who had lost his young wife some years back.

Had Ġorġ Muscat been able to choose his own funeral, he would have preferred to be buried at sea among the waves where he had spent most of his life; the same waves that had seen him dying.
He wouldn't have liked to be buried in church. Too many people. His life had been a frugal one of little money and few friends; so would have been his departure.

Had he been given the choice, he would have liked a quiet ceremony with nobody but his family: his mother, his brother and his only son. Had his Anna Marija still been alive, he would have liked her to be there too. But nobody else. Not the personalities of the island; not his distant relatives and not even the other fishermen of the port.
He would have done without a priest too. He wanted God to be there and God needed no intermediaries.

As the quartet started descending the flight of stairs that led down to the road, a fifth person took hold of the coffin, then a sixth, and eventually Ġorġ Muscat's mortal remains were carried by many hands before being ultimately placed inside the hearse.

It is said that at funerals death lurks searching for its next victim. That's why it is a tradition for mourners to dress alike in sombre colours, not to lure the evil eye.

So, all the women wore dark clothes and black shawls. Most held their best rosary beads in their hands and murmured prayers or passed comments in hushed tones.
The men walked next to them, more silent and sombre, with their faces shaved and their hair properly combed. They too wore dark jackets and their pair of good shoes. Between their hands, they held their hats, which they shifted from hand to hand like a cup of hot coffee on a winter day.
They all walked with the same, slow pace, with their eyes low and their expression grave.

Some of the women wept, others pretended to.

Among the ones who cried, was Ġorġ Muscat's mother, whose quiet sob blended into the marching noise and died in a white handkerchief.

CHAPTER 29

CEREMONIES.

I've never been good with ceremonies.

When my mother died, over thirty years ago now, I didn't go to her funeral. At the time I thought I wasn't going as I hadn't been at my father's either and that somehow I felt it wasn't right to go to one and not the other.

Before that, when I was still young, I missed my own graduation; I lied and told everyone I had a fever.

Later on, I was absent frin both my sisters' weddings. I was abroad. On both occasions, for the family portrait, my mum held a photograph of me between herself and my father.

Years later I almost missed my own wedding. I was late, so late, that my future brother-in-law had begun looking for me all over the island.

The one ceremony I didn't miss was my wife's funeral. I cried so much that I wished I hadn't been there at all.

Why should such deep feeling be shared with so many other people, most of them just pretending to be sad, but not really caring.

The fact is, I never liked funerals, nor weddings or births. I don't like handshaking celebrations or clapping events. I hate soppy goodbyes and official presentations and where I can, I try to avoid any family meeting with more than three people present.

That's why I didn't go to the funeral of Ġorġ Muscat. All those people hypocritically pretending to be touched but really present to just see and be seen.

Instead, I went to *the Club.* I met with the barman and played a few hands of solitaire with my good deck of cards.

After all, I barely knew Ġorġ Muscat.
I had seen him in town selling fish at the market. He was a man one could easily forget.

Funerals remind people of their fragility, of the fact we're not here to stay and that once our part is over we're no longer needed.

CHAPTER 30

AT THE USUAL PLACE.

Kelb was the only fisherman in the bay not to attend the funeral. He remained at home waiting for a phone call.
When at six o'clock in the afternoon the phone finally rang, he picked up the receiver as fast as he could manage.
"*Domani notte, al solito posto.* Tomorrow night at the usual place." muttered the voice.
"*Va bene!* Fine!" replied Kelb.

There were no further words, the line went dead.

After five years, Kelb had learnt that that kind of call invariably arrived five days after the goods' collection. The location always remained the same: "the usual place", a quiet and secluded section of the coast known locally as *Reqqa Point.*

As Kelb positioned the receiver back in its cradle, his finger betrayed a twitch of nervousness.
He didn't like this part of the business. He actually no longer liked any of it at all. He would have rather gone back to smuggling cigarettes, which was safer and harmed no one. Drug smuggling was a much bigger business, meant for tougher people than him. But there was no way out. It was not like a government job where he could just give notice and walk out without consequences. By now, he knew too much and quitting

had become a matter of life or death. Possibly, just of death.

Not far from *Reqqa Point*, the little bay of *Xwejni* was a quiet little inlet set between a white, wind-sculptured rock-formation and the geometrically designed chessboard of saltpans carved into the weathered limestone.
In the summer months, the white veils of the Salesian nuns dotted the bay, as their summer residence was close by.
In winter, besides the occasional tourist who ventured over to see the saltpans, the bay was visited only by anglers and by couples looking for a little romance.

On the side of the bay, carved into the limestone were five caves, one of which was in use as a boathouse.

That same boathouse had been where Kelb had first started his smuggling career.

In 1962, Kelb was a twenty-year old farmhand with little knowledge about the sea and none about smuggling.
He worked on the limits of Xagħra village, picking tomatoes, oranges, olives or whatever the season produced. He hated his job. Having to toil under the scorching sun for most of the day for a handful of coins, was not what he wanted to do.
So when a friend mentioned that the cigarette smuggler was looking for someone to help him Kelb didn't hesitate.

“Can I work with you?” young Kelb had asked the seasoned smuggler.
Frank Xerri was sitting on a wooden chair at the entrance of the shed, with a cigarette dangling from his lips and a pair of pliers in his left hand.
“So, you want to work with me?”
“What's the worst thing you have done in your life?” Xerri had asked the young Kelb.

“I beat up a priest.” Kelb had replied with a smirk on his lips.
“Holy Mary!” Xerri looked at the skinny young man before him and smirked. “Beaten a priest? Not bad!” he said shaking his head in disbelief.
“So, do you think you have enough balls for the job?” he asked.
Kelb had nodded. “Yes”
“Get a chair from inside, and sit down.” Then, putting a hook between his lips, he had asked, “You want a cigarette?”
“Sure” replied Kelb with a smile.
“I bet you do,” smiled Xerri handing over the open packet. “Have one. This is the last cigarette you'll be getting for free. The next ones you will have to earn.”

The boathouse no longer belonged to Xerri. After his death his brother had sold it to Ġorġ and Karmenu Muscat who rarely used it.

Since Xerri’s time, little had changed. The large wooden door was still painted in the same green, and the small window carved into the rock was still sealed with the same corrugated sheet of iron which Kelb himself had fitted on a night of strong wind.

The door lock had never been changed either and using a copy of the original key, Kelb still occasionally used the boathouse to hide the goods he smuggled.

The room had no electricity and as Kelb closed the wooden door behind him he was plunged into darkness.
Kelb waited for his eyes to get used to the feeble glow passing through the corners of the door then realised that the old dinghy, which had once belonged to Xerri, had been moved from its usual position in the back corner to the centre of the boathouse.
Alarm bells rang in his head and his heartbeat accelerated as he took the torchlight and scurried towards the inner part of the cave.

He realised with a sigh of relief, the box containing the drugs was still in its place, yet something was wrong. The net and some of the objects next to the box had been moved.
He hurriedly reached for the box.

"Shit!" he shouted.
It was empty. The drugs were gone.

CHAPTER 31

THE FOOTBALL MATCH.

May 1945.

When Karmenu arrived at the football pitch the match had already started. The game was a confused battle with big clouds of dust rising up from the ground and hiding the ball from everyone's eyes. Karmenu walked to the side of the pitch, sat on one of the limestone walls and waited for someone to notice him.

The pitch was small and dusty. It lay engulfed between two large houses, high enough to cast a large shadow across most of the field yet low enough for the ball to occasionally land on one of the roofs.
On the third and fourth side, the little football ground was sealed off by rusty and frayed metal netting and by a high wall.
Kids of all ages entered the ground either by crawling beneath the net or climbing over the opposite wall.

The pitch itself was actually a building site cleared many years earlier by an Italian company planning to develop a hotel. Some people swore it had been Mussolini himself who had chosen the location.

Eventually the war had broken out, Italians had become the enemy and works had never started.

The site was less than fifty yards long and thirty wide with goal posts consisting of limestone slabs set five steps apart; yet for most of the children, it was the best football ground on the island.

Sitting on top of the stone wall, Karmenu's eyes roamed the field in silence.
He watched the eleven players running in the field and wondered if they would allow him to play.
They played five against six; boys with T-shirts against those without.
Karmenu knew all of them; they were all Ġorġ's friends. All, except Tonio Borġ.
Tonio was friends with nobody. He was sixteen years old, six-feet tall and was known to be the biggest bully in the bay.

"Hi Karm, you want to play?" asked one of the boys. His name was Spiru and he was Ġorġ's best friend.
Karmenu nodded.
"Stop!" shouted Spiru to the rest of the players "Karmenu wants to play too."
There was a moment of confusion before the ball was shot vigorously against the wall.

"What's the score?" shouted someone.
"Two-one for us!" came the response.
Karmenu remained at the side of the field until Spiru gestured him to move closer.
"How is Ġorġ?" asked one of the boys.
"Much better!" replied Karmenu thinking of Ġorġ's face which, until a few days earlier, had been full of the itchy red spots of chicken pox.

"Without your brother you cannot play!" said a voice louder than the others.
Karmenu didn't need to recognise the voice to know that such comment could only come from Beef-face Tonio.

“He can play with us,” said Spiru, ignoring Tonio's remark.
The bully looked at Spiru with an intimidating gaze, but said nothing. There was a rivalry between the two of them.

On the football ground Spiru was king. He was the most talented football player in the bay, and many argued that he would become the best footballer the island had ever seen. He had amazing dribbling, a strong shot and the best technique a thirteen-year old could ever have.

“That's not fair. You are already winning.” cried Nisju, who was in Tonio's team.
“But we are one man less!” replied Spiru.
“He can play as goalkeeper.” suggested someone else in Tonio's team, knowing that Karmenu was as bad between the posts as he was on the field.
“No” protested Spiru “we will rotate as we always do.” Saying so he then took Karmenu by the arm and gestured that he should follow him.

The discussion went on a little longer. Tonio didn't like the idea of Spiru's team getting an extra player, so it was eventually decided that two other players would switch teams to better balance the two sides.

“Who cares?” boasted Tonio, wanting to have the last word “Let him play with you, he’s no good anyway!”

The new game started soon after and immediately Karmenu was tackled hard by Tonio who obviously had something to prove.

Twenty minutes later, Spiru's team was leading by two goals.

Beef-face Tonio was not happy about the score. His dissatisfaction was evident in the way he shouted at his team to play better, to move faster and not to just roam around the ground. "I am playing with a bunch of idiots!", he shouted, or "C'mon, you puftas, *can't you shoot straight?".*

The game might have ended without incidents had Karmenu not scored the very last goal.

Spiru had dribbled past half of the opposing team before skilfully passing the ball to Karmenu, leaving him alone in front of the goalkeeper.

The goalkeeper of the moment was Tonio himself, who with his size alone covered half the goalmouth.

Karmenu shot with his head down, squeezing his eyes at the moment of impact. The bumpy leather ball covered the small distance that separated Karmenu from the goal and hit Tonio's right shin before hitting the wall behind the goal.

"Goal!" somebody yelled from the side of the pitch. It was Ġorġ.

Recognising his brother's voice, Karmenu turned to cheer in his direction.

He just had time to raise his hands in the air before he felt a strong blow hit him just above his right ear. Without knowing what had hit him, he fell to the ground.

For a moment the world blacked out, then Karmenu slowly opened his eyes to find Tonio towering above him.

"Leave him alone", shouted Ġorġ.

The second blow arrived as unexpectedly as the first. It was a kick and it caught Karmenu on his back.

Then Ġorġ was onto Tonio.

"Leave him alone" he said, pushing him. And though the bully was several inches taller, Ġorġ's eyes betrayed no fear.
Soon after, they were facing each other like boxers in a ring.

It was Tonio who moved first swinging his arm to aim at Ġorġ's head. There was a hushed silence as everyone held his breath waiting for the blow to knock Ġorġ's head off and for it to smash on the ground like an overripe watermelon, but Ġorġ ducked at the last moment and rapidly swung his response straight onto Tonio's nose. Karmenu had never seen his brother punching anyone with such force. Yet, the giant barely moved.
Instead, Tonio grimaced and charged straight onto his opponent's body.
He knew what he was doing, as picking fights was his hobby. He charged like a bull, head down and shoulders curved.

Ġorġ was swung in the air and fell hard onto the ground. Immediately, Tonio was over him, squashing him beneath his heavy body.

It was Spiru who finally tried to intervene. His hand grabbing Tonio's shoulder.
"Stop, you stupid bull!" he shouted "Stop it! You made your point!"
But the sixteen-year-old seemed not to hear Spiru's provocation. Tonio shrugged him off and went on to punch Ġorġ once more.
Ġorġ's head bounced onto the ground with a dull thud, then Tonio grabbed him around the waist and crotch and lifted him into the air.

They looked like David and Goliath, but with David about to lose.

There was a moment of hesitation, then the little crowd parted and Ġorġ crashed to the ground.

The moment he hit the ground, Karmenu decided he could no longer just watch. With his fists clenched he moved through the other boys with a determination he didn't know he had.
He slipped through the little crowd and threw himself onto Tonio, grabbing his right leg. With his arms wrapped around the bully's calf, he tried to force him to the ground. Then, without giving it a second thought, he sank his teeth into his thigh.

He was still sinking his teeth deeper into the bully's flesh when he heard a loud shout like the cry of a wounded dog.
With a burst of pride he felt like a moray sinking its teeth in its prey.

A moment later a punch connected with the side of his temple, just above his left eye.
His vision blurred but his teeth remained clenched.
Then a second, stronger punch reached him in the same place as the first.
He fainted.

It took several minutes for Karmenu to regain consciousness. He tried to open his eyes but thick dry blood clogged his left eyelid.
Through his right eye he found Ġorġ looking down at him. His face was swollen, his hair white with dust and his upper lip cut. Next to him was Spiru. There was no one else; the rest had gone. All of them, even Tonio.
"He hit you with a rock. Bloody coward!"

Lying in a hospital bed, Karmenu pretended to be asleep.

"He can't even defend himself!" his father muttered to his mother.

Then the doctor arrived.
He was an English doctor with white hair and a round face full of wrinkles and moles.
"His left eye has been damaged," he said talking to Karmenu's parents, "it is possible that he might never be able to see from it again. He'll certainly be left with a visible scar."

Karmenu's mother was the first to cry, then came Karmenu's tears; at first silent, then louder.
"Shut up, you girly!" said his father, his tone annoyed more than angry, "The one time you go somewhere without your brother and look what happens!"

Then the doctor intervened.
"You are a strong lad," he said, in obvious contradiction to the father's words. "I bet you gave the other boy a good thrashing." he smiled, gently.
"You will have to wear a patch on your eye for a few days. If your vision doesn't come back, we'll see what we can do. Just don't worry too much. Admiral Nelson was blind from one eye but that didn't prevent him from becoming one of the finest admirals that the world ever saw."
Karmenu smiled.

CHAPTER 32

THE SECRET.

The old cemetery in the village of Xagħra was built halfway across the hill. A bronze statue dedicated to the victims of World War II, divided it into two parts, a new area crammed with white marble, freshly cut flowers and colour photographs and an older part, whose timeworn gravestones and fading names stood abandoned, silent, and almost forgotten.

The grave where Ġorġ had been buried was a family one; a plain slab of white marble with no frills or ornaments other than the names and the photographs of the people it contained.

As Ġorġ Muscat's funeral ended, only a handful of people were left in the cemetery. Mourning women, wrapped in black veils of prayers and grief, and silent men wearing hard faces and gloomy eyes.
They too eventually left.

Left alone, Karmenu knelt on the family tombstone and with the softest touch, he kissed the tip of his fingers and passed them to the only ceramic photograph left on the white tombstone.
The black and white photograph of the only woman Karmenu had ever loved.

"You have always loved her, haven't you?" said the voice of his brother, calm and soothing.

Karmenu nodded and looked again at the photograph. It was not the best picture he had seen of her. Its sharpness had faded through the years and its dark tones had slowly shifted to grey.
In the picture, Anna Marija, his brother's wife, appeared sad and distant. Her long hair was tied at the back leaving the delicate line of her jaw and her ears visible in a way they rarely were. Even more, her face and neck were paler than they had been during her life; an ashen, white colour, which turned her eyes into grave and joyless pits.

“I don't think I ever looked at that picture as much as you are doing now, Karm.” said Ġorġ “It makes me wonder if maybe you would have loved her better than I ever did.”

Karmenu said nothing. What could he say? Wasn't it all so obvious?

“I loved her, Karm.” said Ġorġ “But at some point she stopped loving me. Something inside her had broken. She once said, ‘the magic is gone’, as if the magic was something she could see and touch. I tried to bring it back but couldn’t.”

“Did you know that I loved her too, Ġorġ?” asked Karmenu.
“Sure I did.” replied Ġorġ in a whisper “I always did. It was undeniable, Karm. I must have realised that you loved her from the first time we’d seen her.” he paused “We even had a fight about her. And maybe that was one of the reasons why I fell in love with her too.”

“One thing you don't know, Ġorġ, is that she loved me too! Seriously, she did.”

There was a brief silence, broken by the distant barking of a dog.

"Is she there?"

In that moment a young couple entered the cemetery dragging a squealing boy.
The moment was gone.
They had a bunch of flowers, which they laid them onto one of the newer tombstones. The young woman kneling before the grave and the man and boy watching her from a few metres away.

Karmenu waited for the family to leave.

Once they'd left he approached the grave again, and kneeling before the tombstone he started praying.

He prayed for Ġorġ.

His eyes looked at the newly placed photograph. So recent that it could have been taken the day he died.
His eyes then browsed the names on the gravestone.
Above Ġorġ and Anna Marija's pictures, there were four names chiselled in the marble.
The names of his grandparents: Carmelo and Maria Muscat, who had died in the space of a week in the month of September 1961, both killed by consumption. They had outlived their two children: Assunta who had died at the age of ten and Raymond, Ġorġ and Karmenu's father, who had died on the 15th of May 1947 at the age of forty-two.

May 1947.

It was like a new beginning.

Ġorġ and Karmenu's father had died a few days earlier, leaving a strange feeling in the air. A gripping sensation which seemed to whisper that now the family man was gone everything was allowed.

Lying on the port's wall, legs and arms spread on the wet, rough surface, the two brothers observed the evening sky.

"We buried him, Karm. He's gone," said Ġorġ looking into Karmenu's frightened eyes, "he'll never be back."
"Never?" asked Karmenu.

"Never." confirmed Ġorġ.

For the first time, Karmenu imagined himself as an adult, with a wife and three or four children, happy and comfortable with himself.

"What will happen now?" he asked a few moments later.
"I don't know," replied Ġorġ, his eyes to the sky.
"I am scared! What if somebody discovers?"
"Nobody will ever know." he said, "It's our secret. I'll carry it to my grave."

Ġorġ had kept his promise and never talked about the circumstances of their father's death.

"Do you remember Karm, how scared you were the day *papa* died? When the boat came back early and he was not on the deck?"
"I thought I'd killed him," said Karmenu.

"That's why your face was so pale. It took me days to convince you that you hadn't."
"Maybe I did kill him after all. Maybe if I hadn't ..."
"Just stop it! It no longer makes any difference."
"That's cause you are dead, Ġorġ. But I have to live with it every day."
"Then just get over it. He always treated you badly, Karm. And nobody can blame you for what you did."
"But was he really a bad man?" asked Karmenu.
"No, not a bad man, just a bad father."
"Maybe not even that, Ġorġ. Maybe he just wanted me to be better than I was. He just wanted me to be a little more like you."
"Karm, it's late, it's time you went home."

CHAPTER 33

COLOURS.

Like almost everyone in the bay, Sarah too had gone to the funeral. She did not believe in crosses and saints and so had not entered the church; she not had worn a black veil nor had she held a rosary bead, but she had observed the ceremony from a distance, as a spectator silently peeking over the crowded road.
The painter in her had imagined the dark mass of people streaming across the canvas in a murmuring blur of dim shades and light walls.

Once the sun had disappeared over the horizon she had walked by the port.

“I saw you at the funeral,” said a voice, bringing her back from her thoughts.
It was the old man she had met in the same place a few days earlier, Fanal.
“Then, I guess I didn't hide very well,” she replied smiling.
The old man laughed.
“I bet it was a heavy coffin.” he said, with his voice between a mumble and a croak.
“Why? It was a normal coffin, wasn't it?”
“Oh, the weight of a coffin has nothing to do with the body. You see, it’s the sins you commit in life that determine the weight of your corpse.”
“You are telling me that the fisherman who died was not a good man?”

“Oh, he was not a bad person. But what he did to his wife? That was bad.”
“What did he do to her?”
“Oh, forget it, I’m just an old man who likes to talk too much.”
Sarah didn’t ask more, it felt impolite.
The old man lifted the blanket he was wearing over his chest and coughed.
“Are you painting something tonight?” he asked as the cough died away.
“I never paint at night, I like colours.”
“If you like sunrises, you must go to Mġarr” said the man. “Do you know Mġarr?”
“You mean where the main harbour is?” asked Sarah.
“Exactly. You should go and paint the boats in the harbour. That's where the nicest boats are.” The old man paused. He moved the cushion that was placed behind his head, then continued “I don't mean the ferries. Those are ugly pieces of metal. They have no soul. I mean the old *dgħajsa*. The old Gozitan boats with sails. There are still a couple of them left. There has never been any boat as nice as them.”
The old man paused to stretch his legs.
“I worked there for thirty years. At that time, the port was completely different from how it is now. And even I was different.” he laughed, “You see me old, but once I was a strong man. Stronger than any of these half-men you see around. But now my strength is all gone, I am just like a pump running out of steam.”

“Where do I find the boats you told me about?” asked Sarah.
“If you go to Mġarr, you will see them. If you don't, just ask any fisherman, they will show you. And if you want an extra suggestion, go early in the morning, you’ll love the sunrise.”

CHAPTER 34

THE LAST DATE.

August 1954.

Three weeks had passed since the night of the party at Ramla beach. Summer had reached its peak, the island had turned dry and the rasping sound of thousands of cicadas had become an integral part of the long and sultry evenings.
Young people went to the beach and to the festas.

Everyone, except Anna Marija.

"Your summer is over!", her father had shouted on their way home from the beach party, and he had meant it, as that had been her last time out of the house.
She was grounded; with only the concessions of going out for the daily mass and to the twice-a-week piano lessons which with the years she had learnt to hate.

Despite her punishment, Anna Marija had not forgotten the night at Ramla Beach. In fact, for the last three weeks, she had thought of little else.
After the first few days of despair, Richard had played on her mind and so had Karmenu and even more, his brother Ġorġ.
What would have happened if she had gone swimming with him? Most probably, her father would not have found her and things would have gone in a very different way. But she hadn't. She had stayed on the beach and was now bound to help her mother in every little chore.

In the past three weeks she felt she must have washed enough clothes to dress an entire regiment. Not to mention the ironing and the cleaning.

With her sisters in Malta and her brothers in Australia, the only breath of fresh air came from her cousin Rita, who occasionally called at the house to bring her news the outside world.

Rita came in the evenings when the whole family sat outside the house and the children played in the street. She passed through the kitchen, took a handful of candies and knocked on Anna Marija's door. From there, they usually moved to the roof, where the air was cooler and where they could look at the stars and gossip about everything and everybody.

Once Rita was gone, Anna Marija's little window on the world was gone too.

"You know who enquired about you?" asked Rita as they stood with their back to the wall watching the stars.

Someone had been asking about her? That was nice.
"Was it Richard?" she whispered, careful not to have the name roll off her tongue too loudly.
In her mind, Richard had reverted to the tall, handsome Englishman she had met in the square of San Ġorġ.
She had pardoned him and even worked out excuses for his disappearance at Ramla Bay.
After all, she had dragged him there almost without asking him. He was a soldier and most probably he had been called very urgently back to barracks.

"So? Is it Richard?" Anna Marija asked again.

Rita smiled, obviously enjoying the temporary power she exerted over her cousin.
"Come on, tell me! Was it Richard or not?" asked Anna Marija for a third time.
Yet her mind had already concluded that it couldn't be him. How would have Richard known that Rita was her cousin?

"I'll tell you if you let me wear the skirt you got for Christmas. The blue one with the white hem."
It was typical of Rita to be asking for something in return. It was unfair, and in this case even more unfair, as Anna Marija liked the skirt in question very much. It was the latest fashion, brought from England by her sister Philomena, and Rita's chubby figure would probably stretch it out of shape.
"But, it doesn't even fit you!" she bawled.
"Ok, ok. No need to shout." said Rita.
There was a moment of tension between the two, then Rita squinted and pulled a funny face; and they both laughed.

"Whatever! I would have told you anyway." she said as her brown eyes returned to normal.
"It was Karmenu" said Rita "you know, the son of the fisherman; the one with the eye like this" she continued, mimicking Karmenu's half-closed eyelid. "He's started working as a milkman now."
Anna Marija felt a twinge of disappointment. Karmenu, she thought, Mr. One Eye.
So, that was the best she could get.
"I see" she uttered with little enthusiasm "thanks for telling me."
"I saw him in Marsalforn," continued Rita, "he was with his brother. Actually they both asked about you. They wanted to know if you would go on a boat ride with them sometime." she paused "I thought it was cute of them."

Anna Marija smiled. The image of Ġorġ, undressing in front of her, sprang before her eyes. She smiled and an involuntary sigh came out of her mouth.
Rita was looking at her, with curious eyes.
"Oh, oh, somebody is going to touch herself tonight!" she said with smiling eyes. Anna Marija stabbed her with a glance.
"Watch your mouth!" she said, trying to sound scandalised, and again they laughed.
That night, Anna Marija's thoughts went back to Richard to their kiss and her hand resting on his swollen penis but eventually moved towards Ġorġ. She saw him on the beach, with his broad shoulders, tanned and muscular, his straight spine with little dimples at the lower end of his back.
Then, thinking about her cousin's words, she moved her hand beneath the thin blanket.
Her fingers slipped down her stomach.
For once it was nice that both her sisters were away.
She thought of Ġorġ's eyes, dark and passionate and imagined kissing his lips, the same way she had kissed and touched Richard while dancing on the sand dunes of Ramla Beach.
Her breath got heavier and a small sound escaped her lips. Her heart started thumping and her body softened.

The following day, Anna Marija stepped out of her piano teacher's house at four o'clock sweating profusely. Though it was a hot day, she had been forced to close even the topmost button of her blouse, so as to avoid Maestro Cefai's lingering eyes peeking at her breast.

She was still grounded and knowing that her father checked her every move, she looked at the church clock and hurried towards home.

Observing the ribbon of shade that followed the streets into every corner, Anna Marija quickened her pace.

"I thought you were never going to come out." said a voice in perfect English.
Anna Marija recognised the voice at once.
She turned around slowly, promptly suppressing the smile that was blossoming over her face.
It was Richard.
There he was, standing right before her; tall and handsome, in his full uniform, with a smile that was hard to ignore.

But Anna Marija knew she had to ignore it.

"Oh, it's you!" she said with a dismissive tone, and turning away from him, she kept walking.
If he really wanted to speak to her, he had to beg her, she thought.

"That's all?" said Richard "You know, I was really hoping for a warmer welcome. Particularly as I have been looking for you for the past three weeks."

Had he really been looking for her?
It was possible. After all in the last three weeks she had been leading the life of a prisoner.

"I had to ask every old lady in town. And you know what they told me? A girl as beautiful as the one you're describing does not exist!" he said mimicking an old woman's voice, "They were wrong, that girl is right in front of me."

He was flattering her now.
Anna Marija smiled but at the same time she hoped he hadn't really been asking about her.

"I waited for you for almost two hours at the beach party in Ramla." she said instead. She could feel the anger rising to her throat.

Richard opened his arms and lifted his shoulders, then without giving any explanation simply muttered "I'm sorry!"

"Well, now it's my turn to be sorry! I have to go! Goodbye! My father is waiting for me." she said, cutting him off.

"Wait for a moment. Give me just a minute," he pleaded following her steps.

"You had a much longer time than that."
The hardness of her own words surprised her. After all, he was asking just for a moment. Maybe he wanted to give an explanation for his behaviour. But, it was too late, she thought, and her father was waiting for her.

"I 'm leaving the island," he said.
The heat, the shade, the street, the anger; all disappeared at once.
Anna Marija didn't know what struck her. She had been trying to push him away and if he was leaving, well, it was better.
But only a part of her wanted Richard to leave.

He is disappearing again, she thought, and felt abandoned once more.

She turned around with her mouth open, speechless, but it was too late to compose herself.

"When?" She asked.
"Thursday I am going back to England."

Two days! That was so soon!

"I came to tell you." he said with resignation in his voice "Good bye, then!"

Anna Marija always cried in these moments. She had cried on the docks of the harbour when both her brothers had left for Australia, she had cried when her elder sister had married and moved to Malta, and had also cried when the visting Queen of England had left the island waving goodbye.
This time, she told herself, she was not going to cry, yet a lump of sorrow already hampered her throat.
She stopped to think for a moment, as a rush of feelings battled inside her head.
"Let's meet on Wednesday night. At midnight right here." she said and gave him one last look as she ran towards her house.

CHAPTER 35

A RAY OF LIGHT.

Grief devours people in different ways.

Dwardu's grief belonged neither to cemeteries or to sacred places. It was a shout that he carried inside and never let out.

Once the funeral was over, he headed back home. It had been a long week, or maybe a never-ending day. A day that had seen him going out to sea in the morning, lose sight of his father by midday, turn him into an orphan by late afternoon and into a murder suspect by the early evening.

When he reached the house he was surprised to see it so dark and empty.

Shaking off his thoughts, he fished in his pocket for the key and was about to open the door when a hand grabbed him by the back of the neck, pushing him forward into the door. He almost smiled thinking of the short and chubby inspector Agius acting as the strong arm of the law. Then came a sudden jerk and his head was thumped onto door's surface. This was too much, he thought, as his body registered the pain.

"Where the fuck is the stuff?" breathed a voice.

'The stuff? What stuff?' thought Dwardu trying to recognise the voice.
Was it one of Agius' men?

"Where is it?" insisted the voice while its owner shoved Dwardu's ribs further onto the doorknob.

Unable to answer the question, Dwardu concentrated on the voice. It was squeaky.

'Was it Kelb?' he wondered.
Sure, it was Kelb's voice; squeaky, nasal and slurred.
Stupid cockroach, what kind of stuff did he think he had?

Yet, the discovery of the voice's owner made Dwardu relax a little, after all Kelb was a crook but as far as he knew he was no heavyweight fighter and Dwardu knew he could have easily turned around and overpowered him.
But his reassurance was short-lived, as the moment he tried to turn around and face the rat, he felt the blade of a knife press against the base of his neck.
"One move and I kill you." Yes it was Kelb, now he was sure.

Dwardu closed his eyes and swallowed. Where the hell was Agius?

"Where the fuck is the stuff?" repeated Kelb once more.

"What stuff? I don't know what you are talking about." gushed Dwardu his anger rising.
"You know!" insisted Kelb with a slight tremble in his voice.

It was then or never, thought Dwardu and tensing his body he prepared to turn around and hit the smuggler.

But just as he was about to twist his elbow onto Kelb's face, a sudden light illuminated them both from above and catching them by surprise.

For a split second nothing happened, then the pressure of the knife loosened and the neighbouring door a step away from them opened unexpectedly.

"Dwardu!" shouted Bebbuxu at the top of his voice, his tone happy and fresh.

Dwardu turned around in time to catch a glimpse of Kelb disappearing behind a corner. He then took a deep breath and looked at the boy who had possibly just saved his life.

As always he was smiling with eyes, eyebrows, cheeks, mouth and chin. A unique smile that was hard to resist.

"When are you taking me with the *dassa*?" asked the boy pronouncing the Maltese word for boat, in his usual syncopated way.
It was the usual question, the one he asked every time they met.

"Soon!" said Dwardu, touching his neck with his hand for any trace of blood.
"Tomorrow?" pressed the boy raising his thick eyebrows.

Dwardu squatted down to match the boy's height.
For an instant his eyes lingered on the boy's deformed shoulder and on the short limb that dangled from beneath its sleeve, then he found the boy's shining eyes, green and constantly happy.

"Tomorrow I cannot." he said, "If the weather is nice, maybe we could go next week.

But the moment he said the words, he knew they were just lies. He winked at the boy then entered his house, closing the door behind him.

He was leaving.

CHAPTER 36

INSPECTOR AGIUS.

There had been just three unsolved murder cases on the island of Gozo in the last hundred years. Two had occurred at the turn of the century, when law enforcement was still under British rule and police stations also acted as post offices and telephone exchanges.
The third case, a more recent one, was the assassination of Pietru Curmi, a forty-two year old chemist from the village of Sannat, killed with a kitchen knife whilst on his way home.

It was the night of 12th of March 1966, and according to the newspapers of the time, the day had been cold and wet with the rain pouring throughout the day and into the night.
Pietru Curmi had worked later than usual that night. He had left the pharmacy at around nine and sheltering under his umbrella, had walked the half mile that separated him from home.

The killer had waited for him next to his house, sitting on a low wall undeterred by the pelting rain.

Pietru Curmi must have passed next to his killer, as from the little evidence found later, the assassin had apparently attacked him from behind, forcing him to the ground. He had then stabbed him, first in the stomach, then in the chest and lastly in the throat.

The victim lost so much blood that despite the torrential rain, there were still red puddles to be seen when the body was found.

The Curmi case had inspired Agius to join the police force.

Six years later Agius investigated his one and only murder case, the murder of the seventeen-year-old schoolboy who'd been killed by a single shot to the chest in a field close to the sea.

It was the second of May 1975, when the body of Ġiġi Bonello was found lying beside a large caper bush in a remote area between the village of Għarb and the cliffs of Wardija. The boy had last been seen two days earlier and news of his disappearance had sparked a search all over the island.
The body was found by a shepherd who had gone straight to the police station followed by his herd of goats.
The young age of the victim and the cruelty of the murder had taken the news to every corner of the island and the police were under pressure to act fast.
'Nobody is safe', ran the headlines of one of the local newspapers. And possibly, nobody was.
But in full hunting season and with no proper weapons regulations, the list of suspects was as long as the sins of a church congregation. Yet nobody seemed to have had a reason to murder the boy.
Many thought it an accident but some things did not square up. For Agius, who was in charge of the investigation, there were two elements that did not conform. One was the calibre of the bullet, which was large enough to kill an elephant, and the other was the location where the body had been found, a remote and desolate part of the island that had neither trees nor hunting grounds.

The truth was buried beneath a layer of dust.

The turning point in the investigation arrived almost a month later, when a necklace belonging to the victim was found amongst the dry grass in a different part of the island.

Elements soon fitted together.

After two more days the murder weapon was found. It lay in a barn, hidden beneath a stack of hay.

The owner of the barn, an old farmer with a leathery face and with long, white sideburns was arrested and questioned.

It was as if he'd been longing for that moment.

He confessed almost immediately.

"I didn't mean to," he said, "I shot him by mistake". He confessed that, afraid of the consequences of what he'd done, he had lifted the lifeless body onto his truck and had dumped him as far away as he could.

"There were two of them. They were destroying my crop", he grumbled. "I asked them to leave. I threatened I would shoot them, but they were laughing and running through the fields, destroying everything."

"I was so angry, I pointed the rifle and shot once, just to frighten them. I didn't even think that the old rifle would work. But as it fired, they immediately stopped laughing. Then one of them fell down."

For days, Agius had wondered why the other boy had never shown up at the police station. Why he had not told the truth and confessed what he knew. Then he remembered one of the victim's classmates; a thin boy with sad eyes who had cried at every question, and everything fell into place.

Agius had imagined the young pair exchanging affection in the field. He was able to picture both faces clearly, as if they both stood before him. He imagined them laughing, maybe whispering words, then freezing at the sound of the old farmer's voice shouting in Maltese. "Min hemm? Who is there?"

He could see them dressing in a rush; pulling up their trousers in a hurry, then running through the golden crop and hopping across the fields, shoes in hand; afraid of being caught, thinking of the shame their affair would bring on themselves and on their families, yet at the same time, laughing, nervously, unconsciously.

Agius imagined the old farmer in his Wellington boots, with his thick sideburns and straw hat, standing outside his barn, bracing his old rifle; eyes wide open, body rigid, and back crooked like an olive tree shaped by the wind.
"I'll shoot!" he must have shouted. But the boys were probably too far away to hear him. Then, one of the boys must have turned and seen him.

One shot; meant to intimidate; the explosion, then the recoil of the rifle and the muffled scream of the enemy; an innocent boy.

When Agius arrived at Dwardu's house, he was a little surprised to find it in darkness, the only light being the low gleam of the dwelling next door. He knocked and eventually Karmenu Muscat peeked out of a window, moved downstairs and opened the door.
He had changed in the last few days. He looked older, frailer and even more defeated than before.
“Is Dwardu with you?” he asked.
Karmenu clicked his tongue “No, I haven't seen him since the funeral.”
He didn't invite him in but stayed by the door, looking at him with his one good eye, glossy from recent tears.
“You know where he's gone?” asked Agius.
Karmenu shrugged. His face looked too miserable to reveal anything other than grief. “I told you he” repeated “I haven't seen him since the funeral.”

Then with a barely perceptible movement, he shifted the door just enough to make it clear that he wanted Agius to leave.
Agius didn't insist, he wished Karmenu goodnight and waited for the door to close behind him.

Had Dwardu Muscat escaped? Was he hiding?

Then his eyes caught a movement in the building next door. Looking up, he saw a boy staring at him with his head resting on his arms.
He knew the boy. Bebbuxu.

Agius wondered how long the boy had been there. Maybe he had seen Dwardu Muscat?
"Hi Christopher, have you seen Dwardu?" he asked using the mellow tone he normally reserved for children half Bebbuxu's age.
"Was Dwardu here?" he tried again.
Bebbuxu's lips parted for a second, his eyes looked straight at him, then his mouth closed again.
If he knew something, thought Agius, he didn't want to say it. He looked at the boy for a few more seconds, then waved goodbye and left.

CHAPTER 37

ESCAPE.

While Agius searched for Dwardu and Dwardu looked for a way to flee the island, Kelb, the shark hunter, paced through his house unable to sleep.

"They'll kill me," he repeated to himself. "They'll kill me." and imagined Nico and Salvatore with their sunglasses, dark, padded jackets and bulky guns pointed at him.

He was desperate. He had one day left to find the drugs. Just twenty-four hours.
Once the day was over, if he didn't show up at the usual place with the drugs, he was as good as dead.

He was terrified. More frightened than when the big white shark had caught his hand and had tried to rip it from his arm, or the day he had returned home to his mother after beating Father Paul. Even more afraid than when he'd seen the floating corpse of Ġorġ Muscat staring at him with vacant eyes.

But where were the drugs?

Dwardu had given him the impression that he really knew nothing about them. But then who had taken them? Karmenu?

He found it hard to think clearly. Maybe the drugs were still in the boathouse? Maybe he'd missed them, or could find a clue to who had taken them.

When twenty minutes later Kelb arrived at the boathouse, he parked his bike just next to the entrance.
He no longer cared who saw him.
He opened the boathouse's door and immediately realised that Xerri's dinghy was missing.
That's when he heard the distant rumble of a boat's engine.

The dinghy, he thought.
Dwardu was escaping with his drugs.

CHAPTER 38

MĠARR.

The night had come and gone.

With the early light of morning, Dwardu had lowered the dinghy into the sea and had started his escape.

As soon as the boat slipped into the water, he realised he was now officially a fugitive. Then the trouble had started.

He had barely travelled a few hundred yards when the dinghy had began taking on water. In a matter of minutes, a good inch of water was swishing all over the bottom of the boat and more was gushing in from a hole hidden somewhere beneath one of the tubes.

Dwardu considered heading back to land and aborting the whole plan. He needed a better boat; a boat that would eventually help him to survive once in Italy. It was too late to return to the port. Agius was probably waiting for him. His best option was to reach the main harbour of Mġarr. There he would scarcely be noticed and the chances of finding a suitable boat were higher. But that meant going half way around the island. Would the dinghy make it that far?

He decided it would, and pulling the rudder towards him he pointed the boat southwards and opened the throttle.

As the boat skirted the coast of the island, Dwardu thought about which boat would be the best. He wanted a small boat, a vessel he could possibly use for work once in Sicily.

It was morning when he entered the port of Mġarr, passing between the two big arms that enclosed the bay. He passed the side of the large ferry and continued towards the centre of the bay where the fishermen's fleet was moored.

There were eight fishing boats secured to the first of the three pontoons.
The first of the row was a white and blue luzzu, a nice fibreglass model covered with green canvas and fitted with an extra outboard engine, which peered out at the back of the boat. It was a nice vessel, nicer than the rest, but the boat Dwardu was after was just next to it. A six metre *caique*, with a flat stern and a low hull. A wooden model, old and sturdy, yet reliable. It was a boat Dwardu knew well as for many years it had been moored in Marsalforn.

He needed only five minutes, he thought. Just enough time to reach the boat, cast off the mooring and leave.
But as Dwardu approached the pontoon and was about to turn the engine off, the dinghy's old motor misfired, crying out a high-pitched shriek which echoed across the port.

Dwardu killed the engine and looked around. Every face in the port was turned towards him.

CHAPTER 39

A SMALL ISLAND.

Inspector Agius was dreaming of having an animated discussion with the village's butcher, when the telephone rang, jerking him into wakefulness.
He lifted the receiver and as soon as he did so, the line went dead. Confused by the sudden awakening and annoyed for not answering the telephone in time, he got out of the bed and went to get a glass of water.

He had just reached the kitchen, when the telephone rang again.

"*Minn hemm*?" he answered.
"*Spettur* Agius, it's Calleja from the police station in Rabat." replied a delicate, almost feminine voice on the opposite side of the telephone line.
"Calleja? It's five fifteen in the morning, what the hell has happened to call me at this time?"
"Sorry *Spettur*" replied Calleja "but you are looking for Dwardu Muscat, aren't you?"
"I am," replied Agius wondering how Calleja could know of Dwardu Muscat's disappearance, when he hadn't yet reported it.
"He is at the port of Mġarr." Calleja said.
"Are you at the port?" asked Agius a little confused.
"No sir," replied Calleja after a small pause "but I've just received a call from my brother-in-law who works at Mġarr Port. One of his colleagues saw Dwardu Muscat arriving at the port on a black dinghy."

That was Gozo, even the stones had ears and eyes!
"When was this?"
"Less than ten minutes ago. I called you immediately after but you didn't answ..."
"Ok, ok. I know." Agius cut him short "One last thing, how the hell did your brother-in-law know that I was looking for Dwardu Muscat?"
"*Spettur*, yesterday evening he was at my house and you know how it is, we talked about the fisherman's death, and one thing led to another ..."
Agius raised his eyes to the sky.
"Ok, stop there, call Sammut, and tell him to meet me in Mġarr, at the fisheries."

CHAPTER 40

WHITE LIES.

It was five o'clock and Sarah could count on her fingers the times in her life when she had been up so early.

By the time the first blue hue had started working its way along the horizon, Sarah had already set up her easel and had started outlining the lights and shades that emerged from the darkness.

She had just finished her first sketch when a loud blast, coming from an approaching dinghy, shattered the silence of the port. The sound was followed by a surreal moment of absolute silence. Then many small noises filled the air again and Sarah noticed how many people had slowly populated the port.

The boat whose engine had torn the silence had then berthed a few yards from her, and to her surprise, Sarah had recognised Dwardu the son of the dead fisherman.

His beard was longer than the last time she'd seen him, and in the soft light of the morning his eyes looked like two black pits.

With her charcoal frozen in mid-air, Sarah looked at the young man and wondered if he normally came to Mġarr early in the morning. Then she realised that he was looking at her, probably wondering the same thing.

"Hello, Dwardu?" she said, pronouncing his name as a question.
Sarah noticed a flicker of surprise in the young man's eyes, then he relaxed.
"Bonġu!" he replied, reaching for a rope, turning his back to her.
How rude!
"I am sorry about your father," said Sarah ignoring his behaviour "and I'm also sorry for the other day," she made a short pause "when I asked you all those questions. I didn't know ..." the words died in her mouth.
For a moment, Sarah thought that the fisherman was going to ignore her, then he turned around, and simply asked "What's your name?"
Sarah smiled. He wasn't too bad after all.
"Sarah." she said with the smile still on her lips. "And your name is Dwardu isn't it?"
He nodded, then stepped from his dinghy into another boat and started checking the tanks beside the engine.
He untied the boat, started the engine and studied her for a moment.
"If anybody asks you, you didn't see me!" he said with his voice just loud enough to reach her above the noise of the engine. Then unexpectedly, he winked, and his lips opened into a friendly smile.

CHAPTER 41

THE CHASE IS ON.

When Agius arrived at the harbour, he found sergeant Sammut leaning against a lamppost and attached to the remaining half of a lit cigarette. He had the sleepy face of a dog that had not rested in weeks. Agius wondered if he'd bite.

"Already here?" said Agius sarcastically.
Sammut didn't fall for it. Without moving his pointy chin, he looked up at his superior and nodded.
The two of them had known each other for many years, more than enough for the inspector to be aware that Sammut was not a morning person.

The day had almost awoken and the sun was peeking over the little island of Comino.

"Have you seen Dwardu Muscat?" asked Agius looking at the port.
"Is it him we are looking for?" asked Sammut in return.
"I thought you knew," said Agius turning around to face him "Anyway, did you see him?"
Sammut dragged heavily on his cigarette, then replied "No" his voice still hoarse.

"Ask around then!"

Sammut had grown up in the port of Mġarr and, though everyone knew he was a policeman, most still considered him one of their own.

Sarah was so focused on her canvas that she didn't notice the roundish figure standing beside her, observing her work.
When she did, she almost screamed.

"*Bonġu!*" she said, using one of the few Maltese expressions she had learned in the past year.
"*Bonġu!*" replied the man.
It was a policeman she had seen around Marsalforn.

"You're Sarah, aren't you?" he said with a slight Australian accent.
Sarah stopped painting and looked at him. He knew her name.

"Please don't stop," said the man hurriedly "I don't want you to miss the sunrise."
Sarah went back to her painting.

"You're a police officer, aren't you?" asked Sarah with her eyes on the painting.
Agius looked at his jacket, then at his shoes then back to Sarah.
"Is it written anywhere?"
Sarah smiled.
"No, actually I've seen you around in your uniform."
"Oh, I see. Nice painting, by the way. I took a drawing course once but I was so hopeless that after two weeks they refunded my money." he laughed.

Sarah laughed too, but when she glanced at him, she found him looking at the sketches she had placed against the wall.
"You must have been here very early to have already made so many sketches," said Agius.

"I was here before dawn." she said, feeling proud of herself.

"Did you see the man who arrived in that dinghy?" He pointed to the black rubber boat moored a few metres away. At that moment Sarah understood what the chat was about, and as if caught red-handed, her breath stopped half way and her hand trembled.

"If anybody asks about me, say you didn't see me."
Was she supposed to lie to a policeman?

She remembered a lecture she had once attended in high school. The teacher had asked the class. "If a friend asked you to lie for him, would you do it?" Then, pointing her finger directly at Sarah he had added. "Miss Middleton, what would you do?" Sarah had reddened and looking down at her desk, had replied, "I don't like to lie."
It was the right answer, she thought, but when a moment later her best friend Lisa had replied to the same question with, "For a real friend I would lie", she had felt somehow naive and childish.

So, had she seen the man that had arrived on the dinghy?

"No, I haven't." she said all in one breath.

Agius picked up one of her sketches and presenting it to her, asked "Would you say you did this sketch more than an hour ago?"

Sarah looked at the drawing.
It showed Dwardu, standing not on the dinghy, but on the boat he had left in.
"Just about an hour ago." she confirmed blushing.
"Thank you." said Agius.

Sarah watched him walk away, then suddenly turn back to her.
"You wouldn't know where he was going?" he asked casually.
"No." said Sarah shaking her head "really, I don't know".
Agius smiled. "Thank you anyway."

Agius found Sammut smoking yet another cigarette.
"He came in with that dinghy and left with Pawlu Busuttil's boat."
"The carpenter?" asked Agius slightly surprised.
"*Iva.* Yes."
"I didn't know he had a boat."
"He uses it on the weekend to catch squid. But he's no good at it."
"Do you know how long ago he left?"
"Forty minutes, or maybe a little more."
"Shit. We've got to move. He'll be well on his way to Sicily by now."
"With Busuttil's boat?" smiled Sammut "It has an old 6.5 litre engine. He'll be lucky if he reaches Sicily before nightfall."
"Your father still has a boat here?"
"My brother has one, but it's just a luzzu."
"Is it faster than Busuttil's boat?"
"That's for sure. In a calm sea it can reach six knots, while the one ..."
"No need to go on about every engine detail. I am clueless. Just get the boat."

CHAPTER 42

RITA'S FAVOUR.

August 1954.

"I need to ask you a favour," said Anna Marija.
Rita smiled.
They were sitting on the roof, gazing at the darkening sky.

"What 'class' of favour is it?" asked Rita.
"How many do you know?"
"I know at least three. Hmm, let me think. There is the innocent one, let's say, the "could you pass me that book", which is plain, simple and no big deal at all.
Then there is the "could you lend me your skirt even if I am two sizes bigger than you" kind of favour; which can be annoying and occasionally irritating. Finally there is the "I'm in deep trouble, lie to my parents and tell them I was with you" kind of favour. And that, in my opinion, is just indecent." Rita paused a moment, then concluded "So, which of these three categories is your favour in?"
Then she smiled with the pride of a teacher who has just clarified the theory of evolution.

"You can have my blue skirt!" offered Anna Marija.
It was something big, realised Rita.
"Great! I knew it. It's the third one, isn't it?"
"Hmm, yes." replied Anna Marija looking down.
It was Tuesday. The previous afternoon Anna Marija had met Richard and since then her mind had been scheming, trying to find a way to fulfil her promise to meet him.

"Come on, shoot, you know you can always count on your cousin Rita."

"Right," said Anna Marija not knowing exactly how to go on. "Tomorrow night, I need you to pretend to be me."
Anna Marija realised immediately that what she had said made no sense. Before Rita could reply she tried to clarify.
"It's just for a few hours. You won't have to do anything."
Rita was looking at her wide eyes, her thick eyebrows raised in surprise.
"I must pretend to be you? Did I hear right?" she said blinking her eyes three or four times in succession. "How am I going to manage that? Look at us, we are not exactly twins, are we?"
"I'm sorry," said Anna Marija disheartened, "I thought you ... let me try to explain better."
She inhaled deeply and looking not at her cousin's eyes but at the air just above her head, she started explaining.
"Yesterday, coming out of my piano lesson, I met Richard." she said.
"You mean the English soldier?" asked Rita, her curiosity increasing.
Anna Marija nodded.
"Yes, him. He is leaving the island on Thursday and I", she paused again, "I promised to meet him on Wednesday night, at midnight."
"You're crazy!" said Rita smiling, but when she parted her lips and opened her eyes wide Anna Marija could swear she could see the thoughts forming in her cousin's head.

"So, what's the plan?" asked Rita in an excited tone. She liked romantic stories and even more, she loved intrigue.
Anna Marija collected her thoughts, then continued.
"Tomorrow night, you will come here as usual," she explained "but when you'll leave, around eleven thirty, instead of going home, you'll loop around the church and come back from the opposite side. Then, before anyone

sees you, you'll slip into the little alley and enter nannu's *house."*
You, you, you! This is not a favour; it's a military plan."
"Shut up and listen" said Anna Marija "Nannu will be asleep at that time and there is no way that he will hear you. Once you are in, go up on the roof, I'll be waiting for you there."
"There is one thing I don't understand. Why do you need me? Why don't you just lower yourself from the window like a character from a book?"
"My mum always comes into my room before going to sleep. She always has, since when we were small. And these days, now that Philomena is away in Malta, she doesn't miss a day."
"You could put some blankets under the sheets."
"She wouldn't fall for that."
"What if she catches me? What am I going to tell her, that I forgot where my house is?"
"Please! Nothing will happen. Once you are wearing my night-dress she will never recognise you. Just make sure you are facing the wall when you hear her steps."
Rita sighed. She enjoyed a little adventure, but this plan was far from watertight.
"Ah, one more problem. How am I going to get in nannu's *house? Doesn't he lock the door when he goes to sleep?"*
"I have a copy of the key!" smiled Anna Marija. "Do you remember last year when I slept there for two weeks? When Philomena was sick with chickenpox? They gave me a spare set of keys. My mum has kept them in the kitchen drawer all this time. This morning, I checked if they were still there and", she smirked, "now I have them."
"Sometimes you scare me," said Rita with a serious expression "Remind me never to lend you any keys."
They both laughed.

On Wednesday afternoon, after sewing the hem of her father's new trousers, Anna Marija shut herself inside her room and, for the last time, tried on the blue and white skirt her sister had brought from England. It fitted her perfectly.

When Rita arrived, the skirt was nicely folded on the bed.
"I prepared it for you." said Anna Marija, pointing at it.
Rita looked at the blue skirt and sat next to it on the bed, following the delicate embroidery with her fingertip.
"I can't take it." she said, her eyes to the ground.
Something was wrong.
"Why not?" asked Anna Marija, unsure whether to welcome the good news or to worry about something still to come.
"I can't help you tonight!" Rita said
"But you promised!" complained Anna Marija.
"I know. I am sorry."
She was crying, Anna Marija realised.
"What's happened?" she asked suddenly worried.
"It's my hand," Rita said showing her dangling, left hand. "I fell, coming here. And now I can't move it!" she cried.
Anna Marija took hold of her cousin's hand. And held it gently before her eyes.
"Does it hurt?" she asked, feeling a mixture of sympathy and disappointment.
She had been preparing for the evening all day and, as much as she was scared to escape from the house, she was excited at the idea of meeting Richard.
"Yes, it hurts." said Rita "it's swollen. Look here."
Anna Marija looked closer at her cousin's hand, but the moment she did so, Rita uttered a loud cry, grabbing her by the waist and wrestling her onto the bed.
Anna Marija found herself captured beneath her cousin's smiling face.
"Got you!" said Rita laughing loudly.

At twenty past eleven, on her way out of the house, Rita passed a small group of relatives chatting outside the main door. She exchanged a few words with them, then waved goodbye and left.

She walked around the first corner, counted up to hundred, then approached her grandfather's house, and using the keys Anna Marija had given her, she opened the door.

Grandpa's house smelt of tobacco and sheep, a strange mixture that reminded her of long childhood afternoons spent playing with beads in the inner yard.

Wasting no time, she tiptoed towards the stone staircase and waited for her grandfather's raucous snoring. She felt like a thief.

Why couldn't Anna Marija just sneak out of her window like every other lover?
Yet, it was exciting.

She mounted the first steps.
Her grandfather's snoring was loud, so loud that the whole house seemed to tremble.
Gosh, she thought, if I ever get married, I'll first make sure my husband doesn't snore.

But as she slowly climbed the stairs tracing the banister with her left hand, something unexpectedly brushed against her legs.
She had already screamed and lost her balance when she remembered Peixu, *her grandfather's tomcat.*
How could she have been so stupid?

The rasping sound of grandpa's snoring had stopped and a dim light was now coming from the second floor.

She hopped a few steps, hoping to get to the door before grandpa could see her, but it was too late.

"Don't move or I shoot!" bellowed her grandfather; his voice reaching her from above.
Rita froze.
"Who are you? What are you doing here?" he bawled.
Rita could see the shiny barrel of her grandfather's rifle pointing right at her.
"It's me Nannu! Rita, Marisa's daughter." shrieked Rita.
The rifle moved up. Rita could see her grandfather's hand trembling.
"You almost killed me with fright!" he said in a softer tone. "What are you doing here in the middle of the night?"
Helping my silly cousin meet up with some Englishman, she felt like saying. Instead she bit her tongue.
"I wanted to play a joke on Anna Marija." she said, relieved to have found an excuse fast enough.
Then came a question she didn't immediately know how to answer.
"Where did you get a key for the house?"

Rita's voice had been so loud that Anna Marija wondered if there was anyone on the island who hadn't heard it.
At midnight, she knew for sure that everything had gone wrong. She sank her head onto the pillow, and resisted the temptation of running out on her own to meet Richard anyway. Then her mother entered the room and she pretended to sleep.

"I know you aren't sleeping, so stop pretending!" barked her mother.

In response, Anna Marija feigned a half yawn, pretending her mother had just woken her up.
"I know what's going on with your cousin. Do you think I'm stupid?" she said squinting her eyes "God only knows why I am not telling your father."
She paced around the room for a few seconds, then continued.
"It's about that boy. Isn't it?" she asked.
"Which boy?" replied Anna Marija trying to sound confused.
"Don't play dumb with me, young girl. You know exactly who I'm talking about, I am talking about l-Ingliż, *the Englishman. The one you went around the Citadel with, and who was waiting for you outside Maestro Cefai's house."*
Anna Marija looked at her mother astonished. How did she know about her meeting outside Maestro Cefai's house?
As if to answer her question, her mother continued.
"You think a tall Englishman going around asking for you goes easily unnoticed?" she paused "Everybody knows . You are the town's gossip. Do you want to know how many neighbours told me that you have been entertaining a tall Englishman outside Maestro Cefai's house?"
"When are you going to learn that every wall in this island has eyes and ears?"

Anna Marija didn't know whether to cry or shout.
"Do you want to know how many?" asked her mother rhetorically. "Five. And who knows how many more will come and tell me tomorrow?"
At that point, Anna Marija started to cry. She didn't care about the views of all those people, but she did care about her mother's opinion.
She buried her face in a cushion and hoped her mother would stop attacking her.
"Don't cry." she said, "Listen to me. You know what people have started saying about you?"

Anna Marija could clearly hear the anger in her mother's voice. "That you are an easy girl who flirts with any boy."

Just as her mother seemed to have finished telling her off, a loud voice arose from the narrow street beside the house.

"Anna Marija" shouted a male voice with an English accent, "come out. I've been waiting an hour for you."

Her mother made the sign of the cross and Anna Marija wished the bed could gobble her up and make her disappear.
Then Richard started reciting a love poem.

> *"A thing of beauty is a joy forever: its loveliness increases; it will never pass into nothingness."*

Anna Marija recognised them as words by Byron. But the beauty of the words was lost in the inebriated tone that pronounced them.
She was embarrassed and wished he'd go away.

The situation became even worse when her father started shouting at Richard who kept repeating that all he wanted was to see Anna Marija one last time.
Eventually the whole street was enjoying the scene with some of the neighbours shouting at Richard to leave. "Go away and take the queen away with you."

Anna Marija's mother looked between her daughter and the window with an awestruck expression, thinking of what the neighbours and possibly the priest would say the following day.
To put an end to all this, Anna Marija walked to the window and opened the shutters.

Hiding the tears that welled in her eyes, she looked at Richard and shouted "Go back to England. I don't want to see you ever again!"

CHAPTER 43

THE CHASE CONTINUES.

For a long time Dwardu didn't look back. Keeping his gaze on the sea, he let his thoughts slip away with the breeze.

When he finally turned around to look at his island, Gozo was floating in the distant horizon, its coast quivering through the waves.

Why was he leaving? An innocent person doesn't escape, he thought.

Then he noticed another boat, still small and far away.

He tried to ignore it but soon looked again, and again, and every time he looked, its shape was slightly bigger.
It was coming for him.

Twenty minutes later the boat was close enough to identfy. Its white fibreglass form, with a red prow and powerful engine fitted to its stern was unmistakable.
Dwardu's blood froze. It was Kelb, and he was closing in fast.

Sitting at the rudder of Pawlu Busuttil's boat, *spettur* Agius scanned the sea.
"See anything?" he asked Sammut, who was looking through a small pair of binoculars.
"Nothing!"

"No, just a moment, I think I saw something." and forcing the binoculars further in his eyesockets, Sammut pointed his finger to an indistinct point out at sea and smiled, showing his crooked front teeth.

Sammut's smile was a rare sight, particularly at that time of the morning.

"There!" he said with an air of certainty in his voice "There are two boats, one next to the other, and I am pretty sure one of them is Dwardu Muscat and the other …"
Agius didn't let him finish the sentence. Two boats?
"Give me that thing!" he said grabbing the binoculars from Sammut's hands.

It took him a while to see something other than sea. Then he caught them. Two boats; two tiny white crumbs on an endless blue tablecloth.
"Jesus Jeremy Christ!" he exclaimed, "You're right! You're damn right."

"I'll shoot!" said Kelb. "Move again and I'll fucking shoot you!"
They were both standing on their respective boats, Kelb holding the gun with both hands and Dwardu with his arms by his sides.

“Where are the drugs?” screamed Kelb, his voice, straight from his throat, gritty and jarring.

Despite his effort to feel in control, he looked like a cornered rat, pale, frantic and dangerous.

Dwardu stared at him, studying him.

“I don’t have the drugs,” he said, with the calm voice of someone who had little to lose.

Kelb was confused.
What the fuck was this fisherman doing? Why wasn't he giving him his drugs? Was he stupid? Didn’t he see he had a gun?
They will kill me, he thought, thinking of Nico and Salvatore.

“Give me my stuff!” he said almost in a cry.
Then his eyes scanned the boat, rapidly traveling across the tarpaulin to the anchor, then onto a familiar grey shoebox, which rested next to Dwardu's feet.
“Give it to me” he said indicating the box with the barrel of the gun.

Dwardu bent forward as if to pick up the box but instead got hold of the anchor and with a sudden twisting movement threw it at Kelb.

Then came the shot.

Both Agius and Sammut heard the shot and looked at each other, then back at the distant boats.

“Is this the maximum speed?” asked Agius.

“Sammut nodded and Agius damned his own stupid sense of honour and justice.

He took the binoculars and observed the distant boats. The two vessels were drifting apart; one moving away to the east and the other remaining in place.

PART IV – Air

CHAPTER 44

CROSSING LINES.

Eight years had passed from the day Anna Marija had last seen Richard. Many things had changed.

July 1962.

The moment Anna Marija stood up from the church steps, everything around her started wobbling; the square, the people, the buildings; even the church itself were wavering before her eyes.
So that's how it feels, she thought, as her eyes tried to nail things back into place.
She waddled a few steps before her knees gave way and suddenly she was on the floor, looking at the leaning statue of Saint Ġorġ.
Saint Ġorġ seemed to look back with his passionate eyes slightly crossed. Anna Marja started laughing. She brought a hand to her mouth and laughed even more.

She had always wondered how it felt to be drunk and found it hard to believe that a glass of alcohol could prevent the body from responding to the brain's commands, distorting reality into a slow moving world. But it was all true.

It was then that she realised that everyone in the square could see her legs and possibly a little more, as her green skirt had crept up leaving her knees and most of her thighs exposed.

She hastened to cover herself before the whole island could see how ugly her legs had become since her pregnancy.

Once she had covered her legs, she pulled herself up and looked around for Rita.
She found her sitting on her backside just a yard behind her, laughing. Her chunky legs crossed in the air and one of her shoes on the ground.
She too had fallen.

Anna Marija's laugh turned into an uncontrollable grunt and her eyes became watery.
She helped her cousin up and pushed her in the direction of the citadel.

"You made a scene!" said Anna Marija giggling.
"Me?" came back Rita opening her eyes wide "Me?" she repeated "What about you? Even Dun Mariano saw your knickers!" she chortled, "You should have seen his face. He was ecstatic."
Anna Marija's smile froze on her face.
"Veru? Is it true?" she asked bringing a hand to her mouth. "Dun Mariano saw me on the ground?"
"Saw you?" Rita chuckled "Not saw you. He was staring at you. He was watching you as if he had never seen a woman before."
She paused a moment and with a thoughtful expression added "And you know what? You probably are the first woman he has ever seen with spread legs in his life." she chuckled again. "You practically deflowered him!"

Rita had always laughed at her own jokes and, inebriated as she was, she found this one irresistible.

"Oh God!" was all Anna Marija could say, not knowing whether to worry or to laugh.

She decided to worry, as Dun Mariano was not only the archpriest of the Basilica but also her mother's most trusted source of information, a backbiter with the ears of a bat and the tongue of a snake.

"He will tell my mother." she exclaimed "Stupid priest! He never looks the other way," she said, shouting louder than she intended to.
"Shhhhhh" shushed Rita. "Do you want to be excommunicated?"
"Oh damn it! Did someone hear me?"
"No." replied Rita shaking her head with extra vehemence "Just Ġuza's grandma and a few dozen other people."
"Anyway, what do you care about your mother? You are a married woman, aren't you? If you really want to worry, you should worry about what your husband will say." she said finishing the sentence with a teasing tone.

But Ġorġ didn't worry her. He would surely have disapproved. He would have thought that getting drunk was not correct behaviour for the mother of a four-year-old child. But he wouldn't have been angry. He was never angry.

Suddenly, she felt stupid. Being drunk in the middle of the Festa! In front of everyone! What had she been thinking?

But was she drunk because she no longer felt happy with her life? Was it because she could no longer feel any love for Ġorġ? Excuses, she thought, just excuses.

Then Rita took hold of her face, placing one hand on each of her cheeks.
"Forget it." she said loudly, almost shouting. "Let's just enjoy ourselves. Who knows when we'll have another night for ourselves?" she paused, then added, "We need some more wine."

"Let's drink it on the terrace at my parents' place" suggested Anna Marija "We could look at the stars and chat like old times."
"Let's get the wine first." replied Rita "we'll decide after."

The wine they bought was red, strong and cheap; it tasted sweet and fruity and it came along with two small, sturdy green glasses which had to be returned to the bar.
"Let's just drink it here" they agreed.
So, they sat on chairs and started chatting about old times.

"Do you remember the Englishman, the one who fell in love with you?" started Rita "The soldier. What was his name? Was it Robert?"
"Richard." said Anna Marija reddening.
"Yes! That one! Richard. What happened to him? Did you ever hear from him?"
"No" she said "nothing".
It was a lie. Anna Marija had received three letters from him. The first had arrived the very summer she had last seen him; just a few days after he had left the island. It

was a three-page thickly written love letter in which he called her "My Maltese flower", not once, but four times. Written in an impeccable classic style, and with a passion in each word that had made Anna Marija cry to read it.

She didn't reply to it.

The second letter had arrived a year later, when she was already married and pregnant with Dwardu. She hadn't read this one, but burnt it without opening it. Too many emotions filled her mind at the time and Richard was simply out of the picture.
She had kept just the stamp bearing the picture of Queen Elizabeth which was a sin to burn.

The third letter was recent. It had arrived just a few weeks earlier. Anna Marija had read it straight away, and cried, shedding more tears than with the first letter.
Again, Richard had called her "My Maltese Flower," and again, he had said he missed her.

> *... I never forgot you, My Maltese Flower. Life has passed by, with days, months and years piling on each other, but when I close my eyes, you are still there, and I miss you ...*

Letters were a personal thing. So personal that Anna Marija felt she could not share them with anyone. Not even with Rita. They were a secret between Richard and herself; and the postman, she thought with a smile.

Anna Marija and Rita talked more. The brass band crossed the square and eventually the crowd started to disperse.

The feast was over, leaving behind a trail of coloured paper, empty glasses and bottles, and the two cousins talking.

When Karmenu showed up, it was almost one o'clock in the morning and the Market Square had emptied of all but a few people.
Anna Marija and Rita saw him before he noticed them. He moved around like a pigeon, walking in one direction and retracing his steps in the opposite one. It was obvious by the way he glanced around that he was searching for her. Ġorġ had asked him to pick her up from the feast as he remained home looking after little Dwardu, who was running a fever.

She was supposed to have waited for Karmenu by the obelisk at midnight but had forgotten or had pretended to. When Karmenu finally saw her, he said nothing about it. There was no reproach, just a faint smile.

"Are you ready to leave?" he asked after greeting them both.
Anna Marija replied that she needed a few more minutes, so Karmenu excused himself and paced away looking at the closed shops and the street cleaners.

"I'll be back by the end of the summer." said Rita as they hugged one other.

They waved each other goodbye, then Anna Marija reached Karmenu in the middle of the square.
"I parked the car down the hill," said Karmenu, and looking at her giddy eyes, he added, "can you make it there?"
Anna Marija nodded.

They walked side by side without talking, following the narrow streets and leaving behind the echoes of their own steps.
Then suddenly, maybe because of the uneven street, Anna Marija's legs softened and she fell to the ground.

When she opened her eyes, Karmenu was holding her.

"Are you all right?" he asked.

His face was so close that Anna Marija could see the thin little wrinkles that rippled the surface of his scar.

Anna Marija closed her eyes and wished to be asleep in her bed. Then a sudden image of Richard's face flooded her mind, like a vision.

She kissed him.

She kissed him with her eyes closed, knowing it was Karmenu, but dreaming that it was Richard.

She pressed her lips against his and opened her mouth. His mouth opened in unison with hers.

How strange it felt to be kissing a man she didn't love. Not a stranger, but the brother of her husband.

The following day, Anna Marija woke up late. Ġorġ had already gone out and young Dwardu was still asleep. She got out of bed with a groan, clutching her head and closing her eyes.
The memories of the previous evening started unfolding through her mind and a sense of guilt began crawling all over her body.
She took a long shower, hoping it would wash away the shame. But though the water brushed away part of the sickness, the shame remained.

She ignored it and went on with her day.
She woke up Dwardu, checked his temperature, washed the laundry and went to hang it on the terrace.

"Mama will be back in a minute," she said to her son, picking up the washtub and moving downstairs.

She had just picked a new load of clothes from the washing basket when someone knocked at the door.
Leaving the tub on the floor, she walked to the door and opened it without asking who it was.
When she saw Karmenu before her, she quivered and almost shut the door.
Why on earth had she kissed him?

She left him hanging at the door, waiting for a word and deciding it was his duty to break the silence first.

Instead, he just looked at her, fragile and weak; one-eyed, with his mouth trembling.

He was crying, she realised.
What kind of a man was he, to kiss the woman he loved and to cry of guilt the following day?

"I have to talk to you," he said eventually.
Anna Marija looked at him. Why had she kissed him?

"I'm sorry," he muttered again, "I'm sorry. I'm sorry."

Why was he sorry? What exactly was he sorry about? It had been her who had kissed him.
She had started it all. It was all her fault. Only her fault, and it was her, not him who was supposed to be sorry.
Instead, almost without realising it, she found herself shouting at him.

"Go away" she shouted. "Go away! I don't want to see you ever again!" she screamed at the top of her voice. Then she slammed the door in his face and crumbled to her knees in tears.

Eventually he left. She heard his steps moving away from the door, but holding her breath she could hear a different noise; a feeble cry that reminded her of a kettle reaching boiling point.
At the end of the corridor, Dwardu was looking at her, frightened and lost.
"Come here" she said in a soft voice "Everything is fine."

CHAPTER 45

PRISON.

Summer 1972.

In 1972, the only juvenile prison in Gozo was a single cell hidden amongst the many paths of the bastions of the old Citadel.
The cell had no window, just a barred door locked by a bolt, which opened onto a dim corridor closed by a second door. At night, the darkness was perfect with not even a speck of light to brighten its stale air.
There was one bed in the cell, a desk and a chair; nothing else. It was a sad place for a fourteen-year-old to be confined, whether he had stabbed a man or not. Yet, with another five weeks still to go before release Dwardu had grown accustomed to the cell. He passed his days building nassi, *and though he was not allowed to have a knife to cut the wood, he managed to strip the cane with a long nail and a stone that one of the guards had given him.*
He received some visitors. A teacher visited him once a day and a priest showed up occasionally, mostly in the afternoons, bringing a large expensive bible with red velvet bookmarks.
"I am not here to teach you anything" he repeated each time "I just want you to open your heart and talk to me about what is going on inside you." But he always ended up doing all of the talking himself. Sometimes Dwardu listened to him, other times he just kept working on his creels.

Occasionally, his father too visited him. When he did, they talked for a few minutes then remained silent for the rest of the time, each of them watching a different patch of the wall.

But the only visit Dwardu looked forward to, was the visit from Maureen, the daughter of barrister Zammit Caruana, the man he had stabbed.
The first time she arrived, she was with her mother, who remained outside the cell.
"Why did you stab him?" were her first words.
Dwardu had taken time before answering.
"I don't know." he had replied. Then after an even longer moment, aware of her dark eyes focused on him, he had added" He should not have mentioned my mother."
"Why, what's so precious about your mother?" she yelled.
Out of the corner of his eye, Dwardu had seen a small frown on the mother's forehead, but had kept his eyes fixed on the girl.
"Everything!" he had replied, solidly, almost aggressively "Besides, she's dead."
The expression on the girl's face had changed so rapidly that Dwardu could see she hadn't known.
Then they had become friends.

The same evening, half way through his sermon, the priest had put down the bible for a moment and said. "I know you met the daughter of Mr. Zammit Caruana. Do you repent for what you did now?"
"No." Dwardu had replied.
The man had insulted him and he had hit him. End of story.

Maureen's visits became regular ones. Her mother was no longer accompanying her.

"Have you ever kissed a girl?" Maureen asked him one day.
"No." replied Dwardu.
She was teasing him and he knew it. She had decided that she would make him fall in love with her and then disappear from his life. It was possibly her way to punish him, he thought.

Yet, the moments he passed with her were the nicest for a long time.
Then, one day, they kissed.

It was the beginning of the end. Maureen visited him one last time, then disappeared.

Kelb's shot had missed its target but had opened a large gap on the side of the boat's hull.
"Open the box!" he had shouted still shaking from his own shot. But to Kelb's dismay, the box had contained no drugs, just a small envelope containing some of Dwardu's savings. Nothing more. Kelb had no interest in it, so he had left.
When Agius reached Dwardu's boat, Kelb was already far away, and when he told him he was under arrest Dwardu offered no resistance.

This time it was a different cell, located in a different part of town; a normal room, rectangular, almost square with straight plastered walls. Before becoming a prison cell it had been the children's room of a normal residence. Its tiny window had been fitted with bars and the entrance with a metal gate. The room had a sink, a bed, a chair, a wooden cross and a little desk made of painted white plywood.

For some time Dwardu lay on the bed. Then he heard the noise of keys.
When the door opened, Karmenu was there, looking shattered and grey like a shadow.
He walked in looking down, "*Nanna* Lola couldn't come," he said, "she promised she'll pray for you."
He proceeded towards the bed and sat next to Dwardu.

"You ate?" he asked.
Dwardu nodded. He had eaten a sandwich brought in by one of the guards.

They remained silent for a while.

"The police said the engine on the *Anna Marija* was working fine. Why didn't you return to the port?"
"The screw was blocked."
"Lies!" burst Karmenu standing up "All lies! The screw was fine. Not one bit of it was out of place."

Dwardu clutched his fists ready to fight but restrained himself.

When Karmenu left, Dwardu settled back onto the bed, and curled into himself. That's when he heard a female voice.
Maureen, thought Dwardu, and with his eyes still closed he smiled. Then the sound of the opening door brought him back to consciousness.
"You have ten minutes," said the guard.
It was followed by a *thank you*, pronounced in a soft, British accent.
Dwardu opened his eyes.
"Hello" said the girl. "I hope I am not disturbing you."

Dwardu focused. It was not Maureen Zammit Caruana but the painter, *l-Ingliża*, the English girl he had seen at the port. But what was she doing there? Did she work for the police?

"What are you doing here?" asked Dwardu surprised.
The girl froze.
"I am sorry." he excused himself "I didn't mean to be rude. It's just ..."
"I came here to give you this," she said opening her satchel to bring out a black and white sketch of a man.
"It's your father, isn't it?"
Dwardu looked at the paper. It was a portrait showing his father sitting by the port repairing a net. His figure was so recognisable that Dwardu smiled. His arched legs, his beard, his hat, everything spoke of him.
"It's him," he confirmed.
"If you want, you can keep it," said Sarah with a jovial expression.
But Dwardu's expression turned serious.
"You know that I am accused of murdering him?"
Sarah's smile froze on her face and her eyes betrayed a qualm of fear.
"Let me guess, you thought they had arrested me for stealing that boat?"
Sarah was silent now.
"Now you are afraid of me."
She nodded.
"I didn't kill him," he said, "it was an accident, we were hit by lightning."
She said nothing.
"You can leave if you want." he said leaning his back against the wall.
There was a moment of hesitation, then Sarah took a deep breath and spoke again.
"I painted you too" she said and without looking at him, she pulled out another paper and turned it towards him

It was one of the sketches she had done at the port.
"You are good." were the only words that came to his mind.
"Thanks."
"My mother liked to draw too. She sketched in her diary sometimes."
"I do that too," said Sarah, "but I don't show them to anyone."
"Why? Are they bad?"
"Some of them are"

"By the way, my name is Dwardu. But I think you already know that. What's your name?"
Sarah smiled.
"I'm Sarah. Nice to meet you, Dwardu."

"There's one last thing," said Sarah "a man asked me to give you this."
One more time she opened her satchel and this time produced a little piece of paper folded in two.

No, not again, thought Dwardu. He then picked the paper from the girl's hands and opened it slowly.

Chapter 46

ANNA MARIJA'S DATE.

September 1954.

The summer had ended and with it the torrid days of August, the long chats with Rita, and even the long hours of Anna Marija's home confinement.
The first autumn rain had wiped it all away.

With the renewed feeling of freedom rushing through her veins, Anna Marija had taken the early bus to Marsalforn for what she believed was going to be the perfect day.
Her companion, a battered edition of the novel Jane Eyre, one of her all-time favourite books, was the perfect match for a perfect day.

She was reading the chapter in which Jane was reprimanded by Mr. Brocklehurst and hoisted on a stool in front of everyone, when a voice reached her from a distant corner of the real world.

"Hello Anna Marija" said the voice.
After a moment of hesitation, Anna Marija lifted her eyes from the book, leaving Jane Eyre facing the clergyman's hostile words.
"Long time no see!"
It was one-eyed Karmenu and his brother Ġorġ.

Returning the greeting, she closed the book keeping her index finger as a bookmark between pages.

Standing before her, Karmenu shifted his balance from foot to foot, embarrassed like a child reciting a Christmas poem. He looked different from the last time she had seen him. His hair had grown that extra inch, enough to cover most of the scar which marred his left eye.

"Ġorġ and I were going out in our boat," he said hesitantly, "we were wondering, if ..." he stuttered, "if you would like to come with us."

Anna Marija looked at him for a moment, then her eyes moved to Ġorġ's more pleasant features.
He was as handsome as she remembered him, yet somehow different: shorter, maybe thinner.
She was surprised to realise that his build was no different from the one of his younger brother.
Even their faces were more similar than she had previously noticed. Their biggest difference was attitude. Whilst Karmenu feared the world Ġorġ acted like he owned it.

"I am not sure," she replied trying to think of an excuse "I came here to read."

There was obvious disappointment in Karmenu's face. Then came Ġorġ's turn to try to convince her. "We will not be out for more than an hour," he said "we would really like you to come."

It was enough.
One hour later, she was leaning out of a moving boat, spewing her guts to sea and wishing she had never accepted their invitation.
She had felt sick since the moment they had left the bay but had said nothing. Ignoring all her symptoms, she had smiled, feeling the most desired girl on the island.

Then, her stomach had started churning and a tide of nausea had flooded her mouth and nose.
By the time they were far enough at sea for all the little white houses to merge into one long building, she was shivering.

The first of the two brothers to worry about her had been Karmenu. He had asked her if she was ok, then had given her a cover for her shoulders and a slice of lemon to nibble on.
Eventually it had been Ġorġ who had made contact. He had hugged her and she had sunk into his arms like a pillow onto a bed.

CHAPTER 47

THE DOWNFALL OF A SHARKMAN.

If the private life of the sea could ever be transposed onto paper, it would talk not about rivers or rain or glaciers or of molecules of oxygen and hydrogen, but of the millions of encounters its waters have shared with creatures of another nature.

Three years had passed since young Kelb had joined Xerri's smuggling activities and their business had grown. Helped by the restrictive policies of the Maltese government, which banned the import of most foreign brands of tobacco, the demand for illegal cigarettes had skyrocketed. Their monthly trip to Sicily had transformed into a weekly run and money had started pouring in as never before.

And although officially, nobody knew where the cigarettes came from, Kelb and Xerri's smuggled tobacco reached every corner of the island. If anyone wanted cheap, foreign cigarettes, they knew where to find them. The two smugglers were the wholesalers and everyone else their clients. They sold cigarettes by box, by carton, by packet and even loose. And as they provided a service, everyone was on their side. To many, they were some kind of Robin Hood, delivering to the masses what the government had forbidden.

The police mostly ignored them. And if an officer ever decided to pay them a visit, there was always a carton of the best brand waiting for him.
Everyone was happy.

But with their business booming, and their trips increasing, Kelb and Xerri soon realised they could no longer rely on having just one vessel. "We gotta buy a second boat", said Xerri, "so we can start splitting the trips."

Kelb's first day alone at sea was a life changing one. For the first time in his adult life, Kelb realised there was something he enjoyed more than money.
The sea that had once frightened him was forgotten. Gone was the vast, unfriendly desert, full of dangers and shifting moods. In its place was now a land of plenitude, full of fish, currents and far-away solitude.

Then came the day that turned Kelb into a local legend.

3rd June 1965

It was early afternoon and the sun was descending on its evening path. The sea was calm and the currents drew highways of glossy water that stretched out towards the line of the horizon.
Kelb had caught seven tuna that day; all similar, all one-foot-long juveniles; small, yet big enough to fetch a good price at the market.
He needed a few more before calling it a day.
So with the last tuna still swishing at his feet, Kelb lowered the line once more and veered the boat into an ample circle. He was surprised when the cable got tugged right away. It was a strong yank, stronger than he had expected.

This one's big, he thought.
Holding the thread, he measured his prey with a quick movement of his wrist, yet the jolt he received back was like nothing he had ever experienced before.
He shrieked in a mix of excitement and anxiety.
Then the whole boat lurched.
His eyes followed the length of the line, gazing worriedly through the surface of the water to find his prey. It was almost a hundred yards from the boat; a ripple then the swell.
A big tuna, he thought, a surge of joy filling his chest. But when the fish surfaced again, he froze.

It was huge, bigger than he'd thought.
The line tensed again and the boat quivered.

Then the fish came closer to the boat and Kelb realised it was not a tuna. It passed right next to the hull, with the line visibly attached to its mouth.

Transfixed, Kelb watched the beast pass next to the boat.
It was the biggest fish he had ever seen in his life. Three, possibly four meters long from head to tail, slender, mighty and fearsome. It was a shark.

Kelb's first thought was to give up the line; to cut the thread that linked him to the monster and free himself from the dangerous beast.

In his mind, it was no longer the shark at risk from his line but his boat at the mercy of the creature.

Instinctively, Kelb threw an open net onto the beast. Maybe he could trap it. But the plan went awry as the net caught on his watch.

Trapped, the shark sank its teeth into the net pulling it, and Kelb, into the water.

Then it suddenly leapt forward, reaching towards Kelb's hand. Its razor-sharp teeth cut through the net but Kelb was fast enough to withdraw his arm before it was too late.

Trembling with fear, Kelb grabbed his harpoon and thrust it into the creature's head without aiming, scared like a cornered rat.

He was lucky. He hit the shark in the left eye and the spear penetrated deep into the animal's brain.

It was the perfect hit. The shark struggled a little longer, then died.

Kelb had been dreaming.
"Where am I?" he wondered waking up.
Following the low line of the ceiling, his sleepy eyes travelled along the plastered wall finding a small, barred window. Where was he?
Searching for a clue, he looked at the white cushion beneath his head, then he saw the simple crucifix made of rope nailed to the wall above the bed.

He remembered.

I am in a safe place.
Yet when he heard a gentle knock on the door, he stiffened and felt the bed creaking beneath his body. He took a long breath and held it whilst the door opened.

"I've brought you some clothes," said the Capuchin priest, standing by the open door.
Kelb opened his eyes and smiled.

The priest was not the same man he had met earlier in the morning; this one was tall and slim, and didn't have a beard.

"My name is Brother Anthony," said the man smiling. "I take care of the kitchen," he explained. While he talked, he laid a bundle of clothes on the wooden chair by the door, "so, if you are hungry, you just have to ask."

Kelb looked at the man's face, then at the clothes. They were his clothes, he realised with surprise, clean and folded, as he had never seen them before.

The friar seemed to notice his gaze.
"Brother Anġlu sent me to your house to pick up some clothes. The keys were in your trousers. Don't worry, I didn't touch anything else," he added with a reassuring smile, "Just the clothes."

"Thank you." said Kelb clearing his throat. "You wouldn't know what time it is?" he asked.

"It's eleven o'clock and the Lord has blessed us with a beautiful day" he said, smiling again. "You have slept over twenty-four hours, you must have really needed it." He gave him a last smile, peaceful and generous, then bowed his head before leaving the room.

Everything was coming back: the night, the escape, the mafia, the convent.

Frightened that a noose was rapidly tightening around his neck, Kelb had passed the night hidden in a small cave by the lighthouse, clutching a gun in one hand and a stone in the other.

In the early morning he had returned to his house but had found *them* waiting for him. Two men, sitting in a Morris Marina parked at the end of the road.

He had considered shooting them but was too afraid. He was no killer.

So, gun in hand, he had run. He had run through the back streets of Marsalforn and into the fields. When he had reached the outskirts of Rabat, his shoes full of mud and his socks full of thorns, he'd been exhausted,.

He had stopped at the Capuchin cloister almost by chance. He had been on his way to the police station, ready to give himself up, to trade his life for protection, but seeing the small church, hidden behind the high wall, he had thought of safety.

After hiding his gun between some stones, he had knocked on the convent's door and waited.

The friar who had opened the door, Brother Anġlu, a chubby, short man, had invited him to come inside before Kelb had uttered a single word.
He had asked him to take off his muddy shoes and had then gestured to him to sit at a table where he offered him an apple.
"Father, I would like to ask for hospitality for a few nights" Kelb had said.

Without asking any questions, Brother Anġlu had accepted.

"Let me show you to your room," he had said lifting himself up from his chair, "I will need to ask you to respect the silence of the cloister. And if you need to talk to someone, you can find me in the sacristy. My name is Brother Anġlu".

When the door of the room opened for a second time, Kelb was getting out of bed, his bare feet just touching the tiled floor.

There was no knocking.

The two men that came in wore no tunics. They were both short, one bald, one hairy, one stocky, the other average build.

Kelb knew immediately that they were the same two men he had seen by his house.
They entered and closed the door behind them.
Kelb looked at them, then at the pile of neatly folded clothes that lay on the wooden chair by the door and his shoulders slumped.

He knew what was coming next.

There were no words; no explanations; no second thoughts. The two men shot him twice at close range, with a silencer; one bullet each; the first in the chest and the other in the face.

CHAPTER 48

RICHARD'S RETURN.

January 1963.

"You are in the wrong place. Anna Marija no longer lives here." said the woman who opened the door. She was in her early fifties, stout and big bosomed and with the angry attitude of a bulldog ready to attack. "Who are you?" she asked studying his face. "Why are you looking for her?"

Richard's return to Gozo had been unplanned.
Nine years had passed, and the dry and barren island that he had left in summer was now green and fertile in its winter clothes.
All around he saw gentle green hills wrapped in necklaces of rubble walls and low-lying limestone villages with church bells chiming in the distance.

He was no longer a soldier. He had left the British Army less than a year after leaving Gozo. Following his father's death, he had taken charge of the family bookshop, a small shop in the centre of town where he also wriote for the local newspaper.
His life was simple. In his free time, he went for long walks in the countryside and in the evening smoked a pipe over a good book. But at night he felt lonely.

His thoughts went often back to the months he had passed abroad, in Cyprus, Egypt and Gozo, but his time for adventure was over.
Inevitably, he thought of Anna Marija, the Gozitan girl with whom he had danced in the moonlight.
Anna Marija had been the only girl he had ever kissed, not much for a man of thirty, but in a melancholic way, he was proud of his limited promiscuity.

Of the girl of his life, he knew little, too little.

He had written to her three times in the last nine years and had never received any answer. All he had were memories and assumptions.
By now she was probably married with children, he thought.

He had to know for sure. That's why he had decided to return to Gozo.

The house, the street, the windows, the door; everything had remained as he remembered it.
"I ... I am an old friend of hers." he said, slightly stuttering, "Could you kindly tell me where I can find her?"
The woman's face seemed to soften a little, then tensed again.
She had to be Anna Marija's mother, thought Richard; the resemblance was astonishing. Their eyes and eyebrows and nose were just the same, but the woman before him was old and plump.
"What do you want from her?" her tone was far from friendly.

Trying his best queen's accent he said, "My name is Richard. I'm from England. I arrived in Gozo last night, I am staying at the Duke Hotel and ..."

He didn't need to say more as the woman had now recognised him and was not happy to see him.
"I know who you are," she said, pointing her finger at him like a sword, "I remember your face." she paused, "How dare you come here? My daughter is a married woman now and wants to have nothing to do with soldiers like you. Pack your bags and go back to where you came from."

Richard was about to tell her he was no longer a soldier, but before he could speak the woman had begun to close the door.
Instinctively he stuck his left foot between the door and the doorframe.
There was a moment of stillness, before the woman started yelling at the top of her voice.
She screamed in Maltese then switched to English.
"I will call the police!" she shouted. "Go away, or I will get you arrested!"
Just like nine years before, people began peeking out of their windows.

"Please, can you just tell Anna Marija that I am staying at the Duke. Room num... Ahhh" he screamed as a heel stamped on his foot. He moved his foot and the door slammed close.

Hopping away, Richard looked up at the window where he had last seen Anna Marija, nine years before.

So she was married, he thought, moving away.

Why had he come? What on earth had he believed?

"Ejja 'l hawn, come over here" whispered the voice.
Richard turned around to find an elderly man wrapped in a brown woollen coat.
"Ejja 'l hawn", he repeated in a more forceful tone, gesturing him to come closer. "Come into the house."

Richard did as he was told.

The house was old and smelt of dust and tobacco, its walls were coarse and grainy and the furniture aged and uneven.
The man walked unsteadily towards the table, then sat down on one of the chairs.
"You shouldn't listen to her, she's gone crazy." he said touching his temple with is index finger "Too much church!" he added, then laughed heartily.

"Sit down," he said gesturing towards one of the chairs around the table. He then hoisted himself back up and stretched himself over to the dresser to reach a bottle of red wine.
"Wine?" he asked filling two glasses.

"You are the English soldier, aren't you?" he said fetching a loose cigarette from his breast pocket. "You made quite a stir the last time you came to this street." he giggled "People talked about you for months."
Then, looking at Richard's puzzled face, he presented himself "I am Anna Marija's grandfather."

For the following hour, they drank red wine and talked.

"Her son is called Dwardu," he said and, not hiding a sense of pride, he added "just like me."

They talked more; about the island and about the wars the man had fought along with the British. Then suddenly his

face saddened and he talked with the urgency of someone that can no longer keep a secret.
"She is not happy," he said.
Richard knew he was talking about Anna Marija
"She hasn't been happy for a long time."

Richard listened.

"She was not born to marry a fisherman," he said almost in tears.

"Can I see her?" ventured Richard.
The man thought about it for a moment.
"I am not sure it's a good idea" he replied. He drank his last sip of wine and putting down the glass, he added "Alright."
"Do you know where Villa Rundle is? It's the garden next to the Hotel where you are staying."
Richard nodded.
"On Thursday, Anna Marija and I will be going for a walk there."
"At what time?" Richard's eyes sparked with joy.
"Be there at four o'clock."

CHAPTER 49

KARMENU'S LAST STRAW.

May 1947.

What the sea gives, the sea takes away.

After a formidably hot summer and an ordinary autumn, the winter season of nineteen-forty-six had been one of the worst the island could remember.

For Ġorġ and Karmenu's father the season had been worse than for others. In late November, his small boat had started taking on more water than he could manually bail, forcing him to bring it in for repairs.
It was a sad moment when the boat was winced up the slipway, spilling water from its planks. With no money to pay for repairs, the boat remained untouched. Month after month, it decayed like an apple left in the sun. And when finally, Raymond Muscat decided it was time to sell it, there was little money to be made from it, enough to cover some old debts but not enough to plug new ones.
With spring came new hope. The winds were changing and a local sinjur, *John Briffa, decided to invest in a new trawler. Raymond Muscat was asked to join the crew and accepted.*

Reaching over 12 metres in length and with its hull newly painted in bright colours, 'Lady Bianca' was the pride of the port.

It was a Sunday morning the first time Karmenu was allowed aboard. Mass had finished an hour earlier and the little port of Marsalforn was a hubbub of fishermen, donkeys-carts and town people visiting the coast.

"Bring those to the boat." ordered Raymond Muscat, pointing to a pile of nets.

The time to play was over. Ġorġ and Karmenu looked in envy at their friends chatting beneath a tamarisk tree, but knew better than to complain and hurried towards the nets.

The "Lady Bianca" was much bigger and mightier than their father's old. The forepeaks were so large that one could have played hide and seek in them.

The brothers picked up two nets each, one in each hand. And while Ġorġ swung the first one over his shoulders and then lifted the other one with his free hand, Karmenu dragged both of them with visible effort.
As they boarded they were met by the smiling face of Pawlu Rapa.
Pawlu, a freckle-face redhead, was the only person on the crew that Karmenu really liked. He was younger than the others, in his early twenties and had a light beard, which made him look like an Irishman. Unlike the rest of the crew, he didn't just ignore Karmenu but often spent time joking with him.
"You are slower than a slug!" he called out.

Karmenu laughed, then, in a change of role, the fisherman brought his right hand to his head and mimiking an English accent, shouted. "Good Morning, Captain Karmenu!"
Karmenu laughed more, then the redheaded man took one of the nets from his hands and swung it over his own shoulder.
"Thank you" said Karmenu trying to match the men's accent with little result.

Once the nets were on board, Karmenu peeked into the cabin to see how it looked. It was bigger than any cabin he had ever seen before.

"Would you like to come with us?" asked Pawlu "We only have to cast the nets. We'll be back in three or four hours."
Karmenu's one good eye sparkled with joy, then darkened.
"Father will not like it." he replied looking first at Pawlu then at Ġorġ, who was examining the boat's helm.
"I can ask him," said Pawlu "I'm sure it is no problem. But only if you want to come."
Karmenu nodded and Pawlu wasted no time.
"Hey," he shouted in the direction of Karmenu's father "can the boy come with us today?"
Raymond Muscat looked at the red-bearded man with unblinking eyes. "If he stays out of the way, he can come. But you are responsible for him."
Pawlu looked at Karmenu and winked. "Welcome aboard, Captain." he said.

"How old are you Karm?" asked Pawlu as he fetched the last net aboard.
"Twelve" Karmenu replied, aware that he looked barely ten.

Then the heavy inboard engine roared and a puff of smoke clouded the left side of the vessel. A moment later, swirls of green water spiralled over the sea's surface and the boat started moving.
Passing the entrance of the port, Karmenu saw Ġorġ sitting by the wall with the other children. He waved and they waved back.

"I bet that today we'll catch a shark!" said Pawlu coming out of the engine compartment.
Karmenu smiled. I hope not, he thought.

The boat had just left the port when Karmenu's father emerged from the hull of the boat, his face completely covered in black dust. His glasses, hair, moustaches and eyelids were all black. There was a roar of laughter from one of the older crew members, then someone shouted "Ġej il-bogeyman! *Here comes the bogeyman!" and everyone laughed.*
Karmenu laughed too. He had never laughed at his father before and had never imagined anyone could make fun of him, but his face was really hilarious.

Cleaning his face with a cloth, Raymond Muscat laughed too, but his sneer froze the moment his eyes noticed his son's laughing face.

"What is the blind one doing here?" he asked wiping his forehead with a cloth.
He had called Karmenu 'the blind one' before but this time there was a clear tinge of anger in his tone.
"You should be with your mother", he shouted.
Karmenu's face reddened as if he'd been slapped.
"But ..." he tried to protest.
Looking away from his father's eyes, he looked for Pawlu and found him on the opposite side of the boat moving towards him.

"Let him stay, Ray!" intervened the redhead "We are only going out for a couple of hours. I'll look after him."
"He can stay if he wants." said another crew member.
"Nobody asked your fucking opinion!" shouted Karmenu's father "He goes back to his mother."
"We are not going back, Ray, just let him stay." insisted the man.

For a moment Karmenu thought the row was over, but it wasn't. His father looked in his direction and with a disgusted expression said "I don't want him here".

It takes courage for a young boy to defend himself against his own father. Karmenu didn't have that courage. With a sinking heart he sized up the distance to the coast, just over one hundred yards, and jumped.

The water was cold and Karmenu let himself sink, heavy as a marble statue. He went down and thought of never resurfacing again.
He eventually did resurface and when he did, he swam without looking back at the boat, crying salty tears no one could see.
They later told him that the moment he had jumped, the whole crew, his father included, had stopped and waited to see him reach the coast.

By the time he touched the shore he had stopped crying, his one good eye stern and resentful, but also strong and calm.
Ġorġ helped him up onto dry land.

"What happened?" he asked.
Karmenu looked at his brother and murmured, "I wish he was dead!"

CHAPTER 50

WHO IS SAM?

After twenty-four hours in prison, Dwardu was told he was allowed to leave.
"You'll need to report back here tomorrow," Agius told him as he walked out of the door.
"Why?" asked Dwardu, his eyes looking straight in the *spettur's* ones.
"Because that's how it works, Dwardu. Without proof, we can only keep you up to twenty-four hours, but we still need to know how your father died, and how he got those chest wounds. Besides," he added "you're also accused of stealing a boat."

Dwardu shrugged his shoulders, as if to imply "whatever you say!", then turned his back to the police officer and walked out of the police station.
He no longer cared. Prison, trial, accusations. It was all too much.

Then he remembered what the English girl had given him, and reaching inside his pocket his fingertips touched a small piece of paper.

He had walked just a few steps when Agius called him.
"Do you want a lift home?"
Realising he had no means of transport Dwardu agreed.

"There is one thing I don't understand," said Agius on the way to Marsalforn.

"Why was Kelb after you? Why did he try to shoot you?"

Dwardu looked at the police inspector and smirked.
"That's two things."
They had been friends once. On Sundays they had often played *boċċi* on the same team and occasionally meeting in the band club they had chatted about football. Now, a fence of barbed wire had grown between them like ivy on an old wall.
"He was looking for something he had lost" said Dwardu.
"Something you had?"
"That he thought I had."
"But you didn't?"
"I didn't."
Dwardu shrugged thinking of the drugs, still waiting in the boathouse, hidden inside an old pair of boots.
"So he followed you with the boat to get back something he thought you had and then tried to kill you when he discovered that you didn't have it?"
"More or less."
"What was it? What was he looking for?"
"You'd better ask him," said Dwardu.
"That's going to be hard." Agius said, slowing the car and almost bringing it to a halt, "he was killed this morning, shot twice; once in the face and once in the chest."

There was a moment of silence as Dwardu gulped some air.

"Whoever shot him might be looking for you," said Agius in a fatherly tone "so, keep your eyes open."

Dwardu didn't stay long at home.
He showered, changed his clothes, opened and closed the empty fridge then went out again.

His thoughts focused on the message that the English girl had give him.

"Who gave it to you?" he asked her.
Then his tone had turned more aggressive: "Did you write it?"
It was a stupid question, as the message was signed with a name that wasn't hers, but he found it hard to think.
He shouted at her. "Who gave it to you?"
Then the guard had arrived, and she had left the cell, frightened and confused.

Dwardu watched the door close, then turned to the paper she had given him.
Written on it were the very last words his mother had entered in her diary. Words that only he was supposed to know. Words his mother had written only three days before her death.

The clouds are getting thicker. I can hear people whispering and eyes spying behind the curtains. I'll leave... I know I will.
I can no longer live the way I do; hiding; with my heart in tears; listening to the sound of the world slipping away and folding onto myself with just the dream of running away.

Dwardu knew those words by heart. He had learnt them many years before, when he was still young; before he set the diary on fire.

But who else could know those words?
Had his father also read the diary, or had his mother written the sentence somewhere else, in a letter maybe, possibly to the English soldier?

The evidence before his eyes made no sense.

Scribbled beneath his mother's words, was a three-letter name that matched neither the English soldier nor his father.
Sam.

Who was Sam?

Was he the man who had rescued him? The man with the white beard?
But who was he? How had he learnt about those words?

He drove across the island, speeding, paying no attention to streets or cars.

Who was Sam? How had he known his mother? How had he learnt those words?

In the village of Nadur, Dwardu parked the car and walked to the bar in the square.
"I'm looking for a man called Sam" he asked "he's got a white beard and looks like a foreigner.

He was lucky. They knew him.
"His house is named 'Destino', it's a white house with light green windows. You cannot miss it!"

Dwardu didn't miss it.

Samuel Strickland lived in a two-storey house overlooking the narrow valley of San Blas.

He walked to its door and found the key in the lock.
He knocked twice; first timidly, then vigorously.
He waited, but there was no answer.

So he listened with his ear close to the green door. He heard just a clock ticking the minutes.

He had waited long enough, he thought, and after glancing down the street, he turned the key and opened the door.
"Sam?" he called. Then he cleared his throat and called again "Hello? Anyone home? Samuel?"
No answer.

He entered.

The house was asleep, ill-lit and with a slight coat of dust that made it look neglected and unoccupied.
The room was crowded with a dark, heavy sofa, matching armchairs, a cupboard, a small tea-table and a clock, large, tall and old-looking.

Dwardu called Sam's name again, but again, no one replied.

He thought of retracing his steps and returning home but his mother's words echoed in his head.

Walking further inside the house Dwardu reached a narrow staircase, which spiralled up to the roof.
Beneath if was a small study with a desk littered with papers, a chair, and an old, dusty fan.

He lifted some of the papers, but put them down immediately. He was going too far, he thought.

He was about to retrace his steps when he noticed a familiar photograph hanging by the side of the desk. It was black and white and framed in simple wood. But the subjects ... he could hardly believe it.
With bewildered eyes, he took a step closer.
The little light that reached the picture from the roof made the photo glisten, enough for it to be clear.

The photograph portrayed a woman holding a child: a young boy in a striped shirt and dark hat.
Dwardu knew the people in the photograph. It was a reproduction of the same photo that had been hanging in his room in Marsalforn for the last fifteen years.

The child in the photograph was himself, and the woman standing by his side was his mother.

"18th of November 1962, Dwardu and me" was the sentence that had been written in his mother's diary beside the photograph. He had taken the image out and framed it before burning the diary.

But why was the same picture hanging on the wall in the house of a man he didn't know?
He couldn't think of any reason.

More doubts started forming in his head. Was it really a coincidence that it had been Sam who saved him from the sea?

And while his mind raced away, his eyes kept looking at the photograph.

It was somehow different.

Dwardu's eyes followed every shadow inside the frame.

The people were the same: his mother and him, but the location had changed. The little beach in Marsalforn looked larger and with fewer buildings behind it, just as it had been in the 1920s. It was strange, as if the two figures had been cut out of their background and placed in a different, older setting.
His mother's hair was different too: curlier and darker.

There were two more photographs hanging on the wall and Dwardu turned to those.
One showed a twenty-year old man with a thin moustache, smoking a pipe by a desk full of papers. His hair was parted over the left ear and his eyes were looking straight into the camera, bright and cocky as a flag fluttering on the highest mast.
The same person was portrayed at a later stage of his life in the next photograph. His moustache had grown into a full beard and his hair was long and grey.
It was Sam.

With the urge to discover more, Dwardu looked at the desk.
There were pens, pencils, rubbers and paper-clips, but mostly there were papers. Stacks of them. Some were handwritten, others typed. There were hundreds of papers.

Dwardu picked a stack of them and started reading.

CHAPTER 51

VILLA RUNDLE.

January 1963

"Tell me something about the book you're reading." asked Anna Marija's grandfather.
Anna Marija smiled. "It's not something you would like," she said.
"Who are you to judge?"
"It's called 'To Kill a Mockingbird'."
"Is it some kind of hunter's manual?" he said in a concerned tone.
Anna Marija laughed. "No, it's about two young children growing up in a place called Alabama."
"What's wrong with that? Why wouldn't I like that?"
"Oh, Nannu. I don't know, but it's a different book from the ones I normally tell you about."
"Do you think I like only mellow stories about young English ladies?"

"Sorry." she said.

It was Thursday afternoon, the day Anna Marija and her grandfather went for a walk through Villa Rundle. It was their once-a-week appointment, a rendezvous they rarely missed.
Four-year-old Dwardu loved this weekly excursion too. For him it was all about chasing lizards, sparrows and cats, which he did with plenty of enthusiasm.

"Alright, you win." said Anna Marija "It's the story of a girl and a boy whose father is a lawyer. The beginning of the book is simply about their normal day-to-day life, about their neighbourhood and their village. Then their father decides to defend a black man and many things suddenly change."
She would have told him the whole story, of Boo and Mrs. Hall and her way of talking, but something caught her attention.

There was a man sitting on one of the park benches looking right at them.
His fair skin made it clear he was a foreigner, as did his clothes; an expensive duffle coat and a tweed hat, rare sightings in Gozo.
He was tall. His hair, mostly hidden underneath the hat was almost blond. In his hand was a closed book, with a hardback cover and golden arabesque ornaments.

His gaze was still on them.

Oh, my God! It was Richard.

The moment their eyes met, he stood up from the bench and started moving towards her.

What was he doing there?

"Hi Anna Marija" he said. His accent was exactly as she remembered it, elegant and refined. "I have been looking for you."

She was dumbfounded.
"Go!" said her grandfather. "I'll stay with the boy."

"Show me where you saw that big spider." she heard him say to Dwardu, leading him away along the path.

Richard was just a step away now, looking at her in disbelief. His hat was gone and suddenly he looked more like the soldier she had known eight years earlier.

She hugged him. She wrapped her arms around him and hugged him without saying a word.
He returned the hug, holding her head tight to his chest.

He smelt of a mixture of tobacco and Marseilles soap. She inhaled deeply.

"Why didn't you ever write back." It was more a statement than a question. He was crying.

"I married the summer after you left" she replied moving away from him and regaining control of herself.

They sat on the bench. Richard moved the book away and made space for Anna Marija to sit closer to him.

He took her hand.
"I missed you," he said.

Anna Marija moved her hand away but replied, "I missed you too."

"Is he your child?" he asked, pointing at Dwardu who was showing something to his nannu *at the end of the path.*
She nodded. "His name is Dwardu. He's four years old."

"He looks like you," said Richard, his blue eyes still glassy with tears.

"He actually looks more like his father," replied Anna Marija, "But what about you? Did you marry? Do you have children?"
"No. Time slipped away without me noticing it," he said giving a melancholic smile.

He had changed, Anna Marija noticed. He was a different man from the cocky soldier she had met eight years earlier, calmer, softer and inevitably more mature.
He had changed physically too. A few white hairs scattered his sideburns and small wrinkles creased around his eyes when he smiled or squinted.
His body too had changed. He was no longer the bony young man she had known. His shoulders had broadened and his stomach had filled out.
He was still handsome, Anna Marija thought, just as he had been eight years earlier.

For a while they talked about books; a neutral topic that put them both at ease.

Then Richard asked" Are you happy?"
It was an unexpected question and Anna Marija shrugged her shoulders; she then shook her head and started to cry.

She wished she could admit that she wasn't happy, that she felt trapped, with no place to escape to. But she couldn't.

"Please, don't cry," Richard comforted, taking her hand in his, "It will be all right!"

"Come with me. Come with me to England." he added in a soft tone.
Anna Marija stopped crying. She closed her eyes and felt a lump forming inside her throat.
"I am pregnant again," she said.
His reply came faster than she expected.
"It doesn't matter," he said, looking into her eyes, "I will look after you both."

"Maaaa" came a quiet cry.
Dwardu stood before them, with an expression of fear on his face.

"Ma" he repeated looking towards the path "nannu D. has fallen."

Richard and Anna Marija ran along the path to find her grandfather laying face down on the ground.

CHAPTER 52

BEFORE THE LIGHTNING.

11th October 1980

The "Anna Marija" jolted with every passing wave.
Hidden beneath the blue layer of the waterproof canvas, Dwardu and his father held on to the boat's inner rim praying for the boat not to capsize.
With the engine out of service and the storm raging over the heads, there was little they could do but wait.

"It was no accident," said Ġorġ suddenly as the boat descended from one of the innumerable waves.
Dwardu did not understand what his father was talking about. What had not been an accident?
He tensed, pushing his feet onto the boat's bottom boards and turned to his father.
"What are you talking about?"
His father took a moment to reply.

"Your mother's death." He said shaking his head and lowering his eyes "It wasn't an accident."
The words seeped through the wetness of Dwardu's thoughts, leaving him in a state of confusion.

Dwardu had been seven years old when his father had explained to him that his mother was dead. He remembered that moment clearly. The woollen sweater his father was wearing, the breadcrumbs scattered on the red

and white tablecloth and this father's nervous hands twitching like a weaving spider.
Then his father had taken a deep breath, "Mummy died, Dwardu," he had said and, with an unexpected touch of poetry, had added "She died when you were four, taken by the waves on a stormy day".

Dwardu had imagined dense, dark clouds hovering over waves as big mountains and in the distance, moving along the rugged coastline, a lonely white figure hunted by the sea.

Over time, others had added to the story.

"It was an accident", Aunt Philomena had said on the day that marked the fifth anniversary of his mother's death, "she must have walked too close to the coastline and ... she must have slipped".

"The sea has taken her away", was nanna Lola's way of saying it.

Except for his father, nobody ever mentioned the word "death" in conjunction with his mother's name, as if the word itself could make her absence more difficult to endure.

Looking straight into his father eyes Dwardu asked
"If it wasn't an accident, how did she die then?"

Ġorġ reply came slowly. "She was upset," he said in a mournful voice.

Then a new wave hit the boat and hurled both men off their seats.
They grasped whatever they could before crashing back onto the thwart.

After a deep breath Dwardu continued.
"What do you mean she was upset? Did you argue?"

"She wanted to leave me, Dwardu," said Ġorġ almost in tears.
He was confessing, Dwardu realised; disclosing something he had kept away from prying eyes for over seventeen years. Revealing a moment he had possibly shared with no one before.

Dwardu looked at the storm and realised there was something more fearful than nature.
Why was his father telling him this? Why now?

"You killed her, is that it?" he said, almost shouting, his words both a question and a statement.

"You killed her!" he shouted again.

He pushed his father into the side of the boat where they both crashed onto the folded nets. They wrestled, then, with the thunder bellowing above them, Dwardu punched out in anger. It was son against father, anger against remorse.

Ġorġ regarded his son and closing his eyes, he shook his head lightly.

He is crying, thought Dwardu, how vile.

"How did she die, then?" Dwardu shouted.

"She took her own life, Dwardu," he said. "She jumped into the waves without uttering a word. She left us both."

Dwardu froze.

"It's not true!" he shouted. "You are a liar!" he said hitting his father in the center of his chest.

As a twinge of pain traveled from chest to brain, Ġorġ's body folded onto his son's fist.
He gasped for air, breathing what felt like mud. He curled up but again his son was over him, this time not to hit him but hold him, wrapping around him like a blanket on a bed.

"The waves took her down so fast," continued Ġorġ, "she disappeared in a moment. I jumped after her, but it was too late."

Having spoken, Ġorġ tried to disengage from his son's embrace but as he did so a trickle of blood flowed from his shirt towards his feet.
A strange feeling of happiness pervaded his mind. He didn't need to look any further to know where the blood came from. He felt his chest pulsing and the wound burning.

The explosion came a moment later. Ġorġ didn't see it arriving. The lightning struck with the sudden violence of a bomb. The water around the boat sizzled and the ear-splitting roar swept past the two men.

The boat jolted, then the water clasped him, taking him away.

CHAPTER 53

BREAKING AWAY.

January 1963.

A seed of doubt had entered Anna Marija's mind, leaving her torn between what she felt was right and what she thought she deserved.
After her grandfather's fainting fit in the park, she had seen Richard just once more. He had waited for her on the way to the grocer.
"You didn't give me an answer," he had said.

She would have loved to escape, to leave everything behind and start anew, but did not feel strong enough to do it.
Her sense of duty and the moral values she had learnt throughout her life pinned her down to Gozo.

She had once heard about a woman from another village who had run away with her Italian lover. She had left her husband and three young children, one who was barely able to walk. It had been a scandal.
At the time, Anna Marija had condemned her, but now she was no longer sure.

But was she able to do the same?
No.

People are like chains, she thought and the closer they are the stronger they become.

They were all chains. Ġorġ, with his calm and his good heart, Dwardu with his innocence and his unconditional love towards her, her parents with their old, moral views, and even the baby who was growing inside her.

Nonetheless, when Ġorġ returned home in the evening, Anna Marija had decided to talk to him.
He hadn't been out at sea that day. The wind had been too strong and the waves too unpredictable, yet he smelt of sea nonetheless, as he always did.
She had once loved that smell as it felt like such an authentic and natural fragrance, but she no longer did.

"Ġorġ, we need to talk," she said.
Ġorġ looked at her and his face clouded. She didn't know how he always knew. He possessed a kind of extra sense.
"Tell me," he said trying to appear relaxed.

She told him everything, without leaving out any details. She mentioned Richard and talked about her doubts. She explained how she felt and how things had changed throughout the years.
She knew she was being cruel but went on.
Ġorġ absorbed everything without saying a word. His eyes to the floor; his lips pursed.
So she launched her assault. "I don't love you any longer." she said spurting out each word as she could no longer keep them inside her.
For a second she felt relieved, as if an enormous weight had been lifted from her chest, then Ġorġ expression changed everything.
His eyes emptied, his shoulders fell.
She had finally managed to hurt him, but it was no victory.
Anna Marija started to cry.

Remorse shows the difference between a cruel person and one that is not.

She looked at her distraught husband and sobbed.
How could she have been so evil?

Suddenly she felt like hugging him and telling him her words had been a mistake, that she still loved him and that nothing had changed.
But once words have been said there is no way to un-say them.

Chapter 54

Sam.

Writing is like sculpting words from a block of imagination. Sentences chisel the story, then characters make it their own.

When I returned home, night had already fallen and the house was dark and quiet.
Dwardu's car was outside my house and, though I could not see him, I knew he was waiting for me.
I walked up the few steps that led to the door slowly, anticipating our encounter.
The door was ajar, with its key still swaying at each whisper of the wind.
I entered the house and a slice of light from the road entered with me, brushing against the wall.
I removed my coat, switched on the small reading lamp by the entrance, then I saw him, sitting on the armchair, in silence, studying me.

How strange for a writer to meet his character.

Dwardu regarded me with an expression that left no doubt, he knew who I was.

The first time I had ever seen Dwardu it had felt like a dream. He was in black and white photograph on the cover of a magazine, repairing a broken net with the patience of an old man.

I must have looked at that picture a million times, studying every line and savouring every detail.

The picture portrayed him just as I had always imagined him, with the same worn out clothes, his skilful hands and the scornful expression I was now observing. It was amazing.

Eventually I had seen him again.
He had crossed my path one night on my way home, running like a forgotten memory. He passed me like a shadow, silent and furtive and had stopped to observe the sea. The strong winds and the complete blackness of the sea had seemed so treacherous and evil to give me shivers; so treacherous and evil to stir my emotion and tingle my imagination.

He was the character I had been looking for and that same night I started writing my novel.

"I knew I'd find you here." I said.
There was a flicker in Dwardu's eyes, but nothing more. He stared at me, his body tense like a predator ready to attack. In his eyes angry and alert.

"You got my message." I said, stating the obvious.

The message was there on the table, half way between us.

But what happened next was something I had not expected.

Dwardu dashed from the armchair, darting in my direction.

Scared, I closed my eyes. I lifted my hands to my face, fearing he might punch me.

He hit me, but not in the face. He shoved me to the ground hitting me on my right shoulder; a contact that felt like a bullet.

I crumbled to the floor, fragile and scared, like a man made of glass; shattered, confused, betrayed.

Before that day, he had never been that real.

As I lay on the floor, I looked at him. At the man I had had moulded into my character at the fisherman that I had saved and then abandoned.

He looked at me one last time and walked out of the door.

CHAPTER 55

KARMENU'S REVENGE.

May 14th 1947.

A week after jumping off the 'Lady Bianca', all that young Karmenu could think about was revenge.
He had had enough. He was thirteen, maybe not an adult yet, but no longer a boy, and as such, he was no longer going to endure his father's abuses and anger. He was ready to settle things once and for all.

He had a plan, a simple idea that required just a little discreet animal and a little luck. He would slip a scorpion in his father's work bag and leave the rest to fate.

He had found the scorpion by chance hidden beneath a stone at the side of the football pitch.
He no longer played football with the rest. His one good eye made the ball look always closer than it really was. On lifting the stone, the little creature had first scurried away then curled its back ready to attack.

Karmenu had scooped it into a metal tin he found nearby.

The idea of using it for his revenge came soon after, on his way home.
He obviously didn't know that Maltese scorpions are far from deadly. With their sting comparable to a bee sting, they are barely more than a nuisance to an adult man.

But destiny was on his side.

1947 had been a bad year for the Gozitan fishermen. The war had crippled the economy and the schools of tuna had disappeared to the south, towards Africa.

The good news arrived at the beginning of May.
"The waters south of Sicily are teeming with fish." said one young fisherman unloading his astounding catch "I've never seen so many fish in my life, so many I could have scooped them up with my hands!"
His words didn't go unnoticed. The news spread quickly through the islands and soon Maltese fishermen were crowding the Italian waters.

And just as the young fisherman had said, the Sicilian waters were teeming with tuna and swordfish.
Enough fish for everyone, yet clashes between Maltese and Italian fleets were inevitable.

In the recent war, Italy had attacked Malta less than twenty-four hours after entering the conflict.
The residual tension between the two nations was easy to ignite. Scuffles were unavoidable.

Nets were plundered or destroyed and floats were cut loose.

Yet, after a year of hardship, the catch was now so good that an occasional skirmish was putting no one off.

Pushed by the heavy inboard engine, the 'Lady Bianca' too was there to share the bonanza. With her were two other smaller vessels following her every move.

On reaching the location, the three boats cut their engines and lowering the purse nets, they had started closing in a circle around the school of fish. The waters gurgled and tails, heads and fins broke the water surface. The men shouted and the fish was hurled on board and crammed into the boats' holds.
Then came the chants of victory, the laughs and the thank-you prayers.

It was late afternoon and they had just finished hoisting the fish when trouble began.

"Taljani! Italians!" *shouted Pawlu, echoed by many others.*

Soon everyone was looking to the north.
Three large Italian vessels were heading directly towards them.

It was as if war had started again.

The Maltese boats hurried their departure. So, with some nets still hanging from the stern and tuna still bleeding on the deck, the Maltese vessels started heading home with no waste of time.
But not everyone aboard agreed with this defensive tactic.

"Let's face them" shouted Raymond Muscat to the rest of the crew. "Let's show these Italian sissies what Maltese men are made of!"
Some agreed, but others complained that there was the fish to protect and their boats, and their lives. So pride had to be stowed away and, sheltering the two smaller vessels, the 'Lady Bianca' hastened its way home.

Yet hurrying was no use. The Sicilian vessels were closing so fast that confrontation was inevitable.

In a matter of minutes the Sicilian boats were so close, the crew of the 'Lady Bianca' could see the Sicilian men gesturing and shouting towards them.

The Maltese men shouted back.

"Figli di puttana!" Sons of a whore, shouted Raymond Muscat addressing them in their own language.

Then came the first shot, which silenced everyone. The bullet pierced the air above the 'Lady Bianca' hissing and landed in the sea.

For Raymond Muscat it was the last straw. He moved inside the cabin and reached for the rifle they kept in a locker.

"You want fire, you get fire" he muttered as he moved out of the cabin and, embracing the rifle, he pointed it towards one of the Italian vessels, the closest one.

He was about to shoot when he felt a little prick on his neck, right between the collar of his shirt and the stock of the rifle, a pinch just like the sting of a bee. Instinctively, his hand reached for the base of his neck.

The second Italian shot was fired in that exact moment, hitting right on target.
Wounded in the chest, with his legs going numb and his lungs out of air, Raymond Muscat fell down on the boat's planks next to his rifle.
He breathed one last breath, then his heart gave up.

There is no moment in life comparable to death.

Raymond Muscat died silently, between a bleeding tuna and a loaded rifle, unaware of his son's vengeance.

EPILOGUE

Once I finished the book, I never saw Dwardu again. His world went on living without me just as mine proceeded without him.

What remained were the memories and a crumpled note.

Occasionally I read it.

The clouds are getting thicker. I can hear people whispering and eyes spying behind the curtains. I'll leave ... I know I will.

The original paper, the one I found in my new house hidden in the cracks of the wall, recited just the same words.
I still have it, somewhere between the pages of a diary. Occasionally I look at it, wondering who had hidden it in the wall. Had it been Anna Marija, Dwardu or maybe Karmenu?

Fanal's death arrived on a December evening.

His son found him lying on his favourite armchair facing the sea, his expression so peaceful that he looked as if he'd fallen asleep.

The funeral, a few days later, was a simple one.
As usual, I didn't go.
I was told that Dwardu and Karmenu Muscat were both there, so as many other fishermen of the port and *spettur* Agius.
Six people carried his coffin, among which was Father Pierre, who later said, it was the heaviest one he had ever carried.

Time passed. Then, one day in April, something happened.

"Hi Sam" called a fresh, young voice behind me.

I recognised the voice straight away and when I turned around, I found Sarah standing before me.

"Hi," I said, almost shyly.

Tucked beneath her arm was a large block of paper.

"Do you remember me?" she said, "we met a long time ago on the cliffs of Ta'Ċenċ. You told me you were writing a novel."

I smiled. Sure I remembered.

"So you came back?" I asked.

"I never left, how could I." she said looking around to the view and shrugging her shoulders.

"I can see you started painting." I said looking at the canvas she had under her arm.

She smiled. “I started after I met you,” she said blushing a little, “and you, did you finish writing your novel?”

“I just did.” I replied.

“Really?” her eyes had the sparkle of a woman in love and I wondered if, finally she had painted Dwardu’s portrait, “Would you tell me the title?”

I nodded. “The Sea of Forgotten Memories.”

ĦAJR (ACKNOWLEDGMENTS)

First and foremost, I'd like to thank Lisanne Krentzlin. Thank you for your patience and your love. This book is dedicated to you and the rest of our little tribe: Jonathan and Patch.

A special thanks goes to Doris Vella. Without you this book would have never seen the light of the day. If this book were a plant, you would be the roots.

Thank you to Rachel Mogg Robinson, Maureen Saguna and Catherine MacDonald for their meticulous work and their priceless advice. You've been the gardeners.
Mogg, you almost broke me, but eventually made me stronger. Thank you. :-)

A thank you to all the people who believed in me and in my writing, among whom: Pierre Debono, Xavier Wambergue, Diego Pantaleo, Naomi Attard, Rob Ricards, Belinda Wijckmans, Andy Hurst, Zuzana Edwards and last but not least, mamma e papà. You've been the rain and the sun.

Finally, thanks to the Island of Gozo; to each rock, each plant, each wave and each person that helped to shape this speck of land into the island I love.

Made in United States
Orlando, FL
16 April 2022